THE NORTH WOODS ADVENTURES OF BOB BAKER

JOHN PLESCIA

outskirts
press

The North Woods Adventures of Bob Baker
All Rights Reserved.
Copyright © 2021 John Plescia
v2.0

This is a work of fiction. Names, characters, businesses, places, events, locales, and incidents are either the products of the author's imagination or used in a fictitious manner. Any resemblance to actual persons, living or dead, or actual events is purely coincidental.

The opinions expressed in this manuscript are solely the opinions of the author and do not represent the opinions or thoughts of the publisher. The author has represented and warranted full ownership and/or legal right to publish all the materials in this book.

This book may not be reproduced, transmitted, or stored in whole or in part by any means, including graphic, electronic, or mechanical without the express written consent of the publisher except in the case of brief quotations embodied in critical articles and reviews.

Outskirts Press, Inc.
http://www.outskirtspress.com

ISBN: 978-1-9772-4572-4

Cover Photo © 2021 www.gettyimages.com. All rights reserved - used with permission.

Illustrations and photographs by Trisha and John Plescia and Patrick Ruesch.
All rights reserved - used with permission.

Outskirts Press and the "OP" logo are trademarks belonging to Outskirts Press, Inc.

PRINTED IN THE UNITED STATES OF AMERICA

This book is dedicated to Charlie and the next generation of outdoor adventurers.

"The motion of all things was a drifting in the heart of the canyon. Sunshine and butterflies drifted in and out among the trees. The hum of the bees and the whisper of the stream were a drifting of sound. And the drifting sound and drifting color seemed to weave together in the making of a delicate and intangible fabric which was the spirit of the place. It was a spirit of peace that was not of death, but of smooth-pulsing life, of quietude that was not silence, of movement that was not action, of repose that was quick with existence without being violent with struggle and travail. The spirit of the place was the spirit of the peace of the living, somnolent with the easement and content of prosperity, and undisturbed by rumors of far wars."

All Gold Canyon
Jack London

INTRODUCTION

This book began as bedtime stories to our young children in Rockford, Illinois. It is a work of fiction, though some of the places and people do exist. I had forgotten about Bob Baker until one of our kids asked, "What ever happened to Bob Baker?" I had not thought about him in years, but their curiosity prompted me to remember the stories and write them down. Our younger two daughters didn't know the stories at all, so I was able to start from the beginning and fill in the remainder. I hope you enjoy.

CONTENTS

1. Heart of a Trapper — 1
2. Hired Hand — 7
3. Wood Piles — 13
4. Trapline — 19
5. Death on the Trail — 29
6. End of the Line — 39
7. Fear of the Unknown — 45
8. Drones — 53
9. Camp Okimachobee — 57
10. New Beginnings — 65
11. Life on the Creek — 75
12. Heart Health — 81
13. Chickens and Eggs — 87
14. Moving Targets — 93
15. Anticipation and Success — 101
16. Culmination Day — 109
17. Things Fall Apart — 129
18. Rest in Pieces — 141
19. Recovery — 153
20. Brother's Keeper — 159

Photograph by Patrick Ruesch

1

HEART OF A TRAPPER

In the far North Woods of Maine there lived an Old Man in a log cabin. He was there all alone except for his faithful dog, Lou. It was bitterly cold, even for the Old Man who had spent many years in the North Woods. His breath froze and turned to crystals as soon as the moisture hit the dry air. Small clumps of ice formed in his gray beard and mustache. Any exposed skin stung on contact with the frosty air. He carefully loaded his supplies into the sled behind his Polaris snowmobile.

"Come here, boy," he called to the old dog. "Climb up here."

The dog always sat behind him on the snowmobile. They headed down the packed trail toward Aspen Pond. Three feet of heavy snow lay on the landscape like a thick, white blanket, indifferent to the creatures beneath. Small trees were covered lumps, large trees were coat racks with white burdens. The pines and birches patiently awaited the morning sun to peek over the horizon. The Old Man eased the snowmobile and sled off the trail and down the gradual embankment to the edge of Aspen Pond. The Old Man grabbed his wood handled ax and headed for the first set.

"Come on, old boy," he said.

The dog was hesitant to vacate the warm snowmobile but enjoyed following his master on the trapline. They had been together since the dog was a pup. The Old Man walked to the first stick protruding through the thick ice and took a few solid chops at the base of the stick. Once the stick was loosened, he pulled upward on it and was happy to find heavy resistance.

"Oh good," he said to the dog, as much as to himself.

He took a few more full swings with the ax to break away a chunk of ice about two feet in diameter. Up through the icy water he pulled the stick with the attached conibear trap that held a large prime male beaver. He placed the beaver and the trap on top of the ice and put the six-foot-tall willow stick next to them. He continued methodically around the shoreline to his similar sets. It took about two hours to gather all ten willow sticks and traps. He was happy with the four beavers that he'd harvested. As he was slowly pulling the beavers and the equipment back to his sled, he grumbled to himself how tired his arms were getting in the blasted cold.

Once the heavy sled was loaded, he fired up the old snowmobile and continued down the trail to Loon Lake. By now it was noon, and he was more than ready to take a break. The Old Man poured himself a cup of hot, pitch black coffee from his thermos and hungrily bit into a roast venison sandwich and sour dough biscuit.

"Here boy," he said, as he tossed a chunk of venison and a stale biscuit to the dog.

The dog looked up at him with droopy, brown eyes as if to ask, *Can we get back to the cabin now*?

"Sorry boy," said the Old Man. "We've got a bit more to do yet."

By now the sun was higher but still low slung in the southern sky. He wiped some of the frost from his gray beard and brought ten traps and poles down to the ice-covered lake. Aspen Pond had been pretty well played out and he was happy with the catch that it had provided. Now he was focused on Loon Lake. He had learned over the years to be a good steward of the land and always leave some seed animals for next year. He worked his way around the north perimeter of the lake, chopping holes in the ice and setting traps. This lake, named after the diving loons, had always produced good furs.

When he had set eight of the ten traps, he muttered to himself, "That's enough," and, somewhat disheartened, put the two unused traps and sticks back into the sled with the frozen beavers. He turned the key on the snowmobile and it sputtered, hesitant to start as strong gasoline fumes permeated the frigid air.

"Dern polar vortex," he grumbled.

When the high-mileage engine finally started, he squeezed the throttle and headed back for the log cabin. By now it was getting toward evening and his old muscles and joints were achy and tired. He pulled the snowmobile into the fur shed and hung up the beavers. Then he slowly headed up the steps to the log cabin and trudged inside. The warm air was close and comforting. He shook off his heavy L.L. Bean coat and sat his boots on the plastic boot rack.

"Oh boy," he said as he rubbed his cold hands together and added kindling to the warm coals in the wood-burning stove.

Flames quickly picked up and soon he had water boiling for his evening tea. The dog curled up on the rug in front of the fire and rested. The Old Man cut slices of venison roast into his black cast iron pan and sliced in some onion with butter, placing it on top of the stove.

After he finished his meal, he sat in the rocking chair facing the crackling fire and wrote in his journal:

December 14th

Why do I feel this way? Tired all the time. I used to be able to work a full day and be fine. Now after a couple hours I'm ready to rest. My back, knees, and shoulders are always tight and sore. The cold gets to me. Why did I think this wouldn't happen to me? I wonder what my boy Ken is doing. He's not a boy anymore, he's nearly the age I was when I moved out here to The County.

The Old Man looked away from his journal. His eyes panned across the wooden floor planks and simple furnishings to the photo on the dusty window sill. A man and woman, pushing a little boy about five years old on a swing at the city park in Allagash. Short sleeves, natural smiles, and green grass. The Old Man shook his head and breathed deep to break from the heavy thoughts. "I'm exhausted," he said to himself, closing the journal. "Goodnight ole Lou."

He fell asleep feeling rather defeated and deflated, but he slept soundly and woke to a sunny morning. Something about refreshing sleep allowed him to form his thoughts and come to a conclusion about what to do. Overall, the Old Man was happy with his life's profession. He always enjoyed his own company and this wild place. He appreciated the quiet, natural splendor of the North Woods, but he knew this would not get any easier. At his age, he found himself wishing he had someone to work with and share the experience.

Photograph by Trisha Plescia

2

HIRED HAND

The next morning the Old Man woke up and hurriedly put more wood on the fire. He retreated to the comfort of his bunk while he waited for the stove to heat the cabin. He boiled water for oatmeal and drank his first cup of coffee as the dog stirred on the rug.

"It's morning, boy. Let's get moving," he said to the dog, patting his head.

The Old Man bundled up and headed out to the fur shed. He skinned the four beavers and admired the thick, luscious pelts. He tacked and stretched the pelts in nice circles and placed them in the corner of the shed to dry. Then he fired up the snowmobile and headed back down the trail to Loon Lake.

The first three sets were empty. The next held a dark, juvenile beaver. He pulled the beaver from the water and reset the trap. The eighth trap on Loon Lake held a large female beaver that would probably bring $40 at auction. The Old Man and his dog packed the sled and headed up to the pines on the south side of the trail. They worked their way through the white pines and spruce, checking the cubby sets for fishers and weasels. He collected two fishers and one beautiful bobcat from the 30-acre pine thicket. He was impressed with the amount of fur he was taking in and knew that with another pair of hands he could be setting many more traps and increasing his catch. They headed back to camp and stopped at the fur shed just long enough to unhitch the sled.

"Hold on tight, Lou, here we go," he said to his four-legged friend as he gunned the engine down the trail in the opposite direction, toward town.

It was ten miles through unspoiled wilderness before he reached the small, snow-covered potato field and gravel lot at the edge of Allagash, Maine. There were two inches of fresh snow from the night before, which blanketed the trees and simple homes. He parked his snowmobile in front of Two Rivers Lunch restaurant and walked up the front steps. He shook off the snow and cold before stepping in the front door.

As the bell above the door chimed, Emma called from behind the counter, "Hey there, old timer. What can I get for you?"

"I'll take a cup of coffee and a bowl of that turkey wild rice soup."

He sat down at the nearest table and read the local paper that was sitting nearby. Emma had grown up in Allagash and the Old Man had known her since she was a little girl. Her parents owned the restaurant and she had been working there since she could see over the counter. He was drinking his coffee when the door opened and Ted Thompson came in.

"Sure is cold, ain't it, Old Man?" said Ted.

Ted pulled up a chair at the table with the Old Man and asked him how things were going out in the woods.

"Can't complain," said the Old Man, "and it wouldn't change anything if I did."

"I hear that," said Ted.

Ted was the local sheriff and had known the Old Man for many years.

"The trapping is actually going pretty well," said the Old Man, between bites of thick, hot, creamy soup. "It just seems to be a lot more work and everything is heavier than it used to be. I'm so exhausted by the end of the day. It takes all my effort to feed the dog and get into bed."

"Well, nobody's gettin' any younger," said Ted. "And it sure ain't easy doin' all the work you do out in those woods Old Man. Shoot, there's plenty of young guys that couldn't keep up with you splittin' logs and putting up furs."

"Maybe so," said the Old Man, "but I'm ready to get a little help out on the line if I can find it. Do you know of anybody looking for work?"

Ted Thompson paused and thought about it for a long moment. "There's my nephew George, or his buddy Terry Tinner," he suggested. The Old Man knew the work ethic of both men and knew that they would not last long in the woods. The Old Man's silence made Ted continue to ponder the options. "Oh wait, well, there's this new fella that just came into town last week. He's been staying down at the hotel playing pool most of the time."

"Oh yeah?" asked the Old Man. "Who is he?"

"Goes by the name of Bob Baker," said Ted. "Pretty quiet,

keeps to himself. Rumor has it he spent some time in prison. Look, you don't want him. You don't wanna have to be watching your back all the time."

"What did he go to prison for?" asked the Old Man.

"I don't know. In fact, it's all just rumors that I've heard. Somebody said he was looking for work. But I wouldn't mess around with him. You never know what kind of character he is coming out of prison. They often learn more dirty tricks in there than they already had going in."

"Hmm... You've heard it before, Ted. Never believe what you hear, and only half of what you see," said the Old Man as he finished his coffee, paid his tab, and headed out the door. As he walked the fifty yards down to the hotel, he thought about this Bob Baker. The folks around town would certainly not understand allowing a stranger into his cabin, especially an ex-con. They'd think he was nuts and irresponsible. The Old Man didn't feel he had much to lose, and besides, he was curious and open-minded.

The lady behind the counter of the quaint hotel, wearing a thick red sweater and her hair in a gray bun, asked, "What can I help you with, Old Man?"

"Well, I'm looking for a fella that goes by the name of Bob Baker."

Suddenly, from the next room came a steady voice beside the pool table, "Who's askin?"

"Howdy, name's Man. Old Man. Pleasure to meet you."

"Hi, I'm Bob Baker," said the man with shaggy brown hair, dark beard, and flannel shirt.

In the Old Man's prime he was as tall as Bob's 5'10," but age had taken him down a good two inches in height and thickness. Bob was a sturdy 180 pounds, with square shoulders and a firm jaw.

"I'm looking for somebody to help me run my trapline. Have you done any trapping before?" asked the Old Man.

"Well," said Bob Baker, with a southern drawl, "I grew up in eastern Kentucky on the family farm. I did my fair share of huntin', fishin', and trappin' at times for spending money when I wasn't digging coal. That was a long time ago. I'm a hard worker and pick up on things quick. I was hoping to find some work and stay around these parts, at least for a while."

"Well I'd be happy to have you," said the Old Man. "The only thing is…" he paused. "You'd have to stay out at my cabin because I'm ten miles out in the woods and we can't waste the time having you drive back and forth."

"That's fine with me," said Bob Baker. "I'd be happy to get out of town."

"Well good," said the Old Man. "I'll pick you up here tomorrow at noon."

"No, that's OK," said Bob Baker. "I'd rather snowshoe it out to your cabin to get a lay of the land."

"Perfect," said the Old Man, as they exchanged a firm handshake.

The Old Man had spent many years reading sign on the trapline and in humans… he liked the shine in Bob Baker's brown eyes.

Photograph by Trisha Plescia

3

WOOD PILES

The next morning was sunny and crisp. At the hotel, Bob had a quick breakfast of steel-cut oatmeal with cream, almonds, and maple syrup. The coffee was inky black and strong. He had his pack loaded down with clothes, extra boots, a few books and journals, a hunting knife, and his .308 slung over his shoulder. He strapped the three-foot, webbed L.L. Bean heritage snowshoes over his wolverine boots, shifted the pack, and headed out.

The sun was off to his right as he walked north. The snow was fresh and powdery, but he was happy to have the snowshoes for buoyance. It felt good to be moving. His lungs pulled in the fresh air and exhaled frozen mist. Bob could feel his legs moving like pistons propelling him forward. He was excited to get out of town and into a new adventure. The Old Man had seemed genuine and easygoing.

The land was gently rolling with dense woods on either side of the trail. It was about twelve feet wide with mostly white pines along each side. He covered three miles before pausing for a breather. The quiet was impressive. A few cardinals and chickadees bounced between branches. Several cumulus clouds shifted slowly across the clear blue sky. He quickly started to feel the chill of cooling sweat, so he started on again. The pack felt good and balanced. He saw few animal tracks and no signs of humans.

Four hours after leaving the hotel, Bob came to a wide spot in the trail and could see snowmobile tracks leading to the east into a clearing. A solid, single story log cabin sat fittingly in the center of the clearing, with smoke curling upward. It was picturesque and natural. The logs were pine and had clearly stood where the meadow was now covered in snow. The workmanship was apparent. The place had been built to last: squared logs, chinked and stacked with utmost care and windows double-paned, the chimney masoned from stones found by the creek that skirted the clearing. When Bob was ten feet from the overhanging porch, a black lab came around the corner of the cabin with warning barks.

"Hey there, boy," said Bob, with his outstretched open hand.

A few licks and tail wags showed that the dog was friendly. He had gray salt-and-pepper in the coarse muzzle hair. The Old Man came around the corner a minute later, showing he appreciated the dog's warning barks.

"Hey Bob," said the Old Man. "I see you've met Lou. He's companion, doorbell, and alarm system all in one."

"I was just admiring the cabin," said Bob.

"It's no luxury mansion, but it keeps me warm and out of the elements. I was just chopping wood out back. Here, set your luggage down and give me a hand."

Bob put his pack, gun, and snowshoes on a neat stack of

wood on the front porch, tucked beneath the overhang. The Old Man handed him a thermos with warm tea.

"How was the walk out?"

"Not bad," said Bob. "Pretty country and lots of quiet."

"Yep, not a bad neighborhood," said the Old Man with a wink.

They went around the back of the cabin and Bob could see a lean-to connected to the back of the building by a narrow doorway. The snow was stamped by boot tracks and broken bark lay scattered about. A pile of aspen logs, about one to two feet each, lay next to a sawbuck, and light sawdust was on the snow.

"Here," said the Old Man. "I'll set them and you can split."

There was a single bit, wood-handled ax and an eight pound maul. Bob grabbed the ax and the Old Man set a two-foot-wide log into the snow and a smaller one on top. Bob swung the ax down and split the log in half. The Old Man put each half on the chopping log again and Bob split them in turn. The Old Man would grab the next log and get it into position, and they'd repeat the process. They worked in this manner for thirty minutes without saying a word. The split wood gathering on either side of the chopping block.

Finally, the Old Man said, "OK, let's stack this."

They brought the chopped birch twenty feet to the covered wood pile. Once that was stacked, the Old Man said, "Now we switch."

Bob set the logs in place and the Old Man swung the ax. Bob was impressed with the strength and easy movement of the Old Man. The pile of sawed logs disappeared, and they stacked the split stuff again. Next, the Old Man fired up the Stihl chainsaw and worked the 18-inch bar into some big cedar branches. Bob hoisted the ten-foot lengths into the sawbuck and the Old Man cut off manageable logs. The sun was slipping away to the west, slung low in the southern sky.

"OK," said the Old Man breathing hard. "We got a lot done. Let's call it a day."

"Sounds good," said Bob Baker.

They put away the equipment and brushed the sawdust off their coveralls before entering the cabin. The inside was simple and cozy. Jars of moose meat and canned vegetables lined the open-faced wooden cupboard. The Old Man showed Bob the slop sink and the big metal pitcher that was sitting on the cast-iron woodburning stove. They washed up with the warm water and soap.

"Ah... feels good to sit," said the Old Man, dropping down onto one of the chairs beside the simple wooden table.

Bob noticed a one-pound package of thawed, ground venison sitting on the counter.

"What's your plan for the meat?" asked Bob.

"I was thinking of pasta and meatballs," said the Old Man.

"Sounds good, I can get that going," replied Bob.

"Sure," said the Old Man. "There are ingredients and pans in the cupboard."

Bob chopped onions and added them to breadcrumbs, an egg, salt, pepper, garlic, and oregano into a mixing bowl with the meat. He used his hands to knead all the ingredients together in the metal bowl. He formed meatballs and carefully dropped them into the cast iron pan atop the woodburning stove. They started to stick to the hot metal, so he added a tablespoon of butter. Next, he added a pound of pasta to the boiling water on the wood burner.

The Old Man rested and pet Lou, who was curled at his side. The aromas were heavenly and both men were hungry after all the calories they had burned during the day. Bob rolled the meatballs until all sides were crispy and browned. When the mostaccioli was soft to fork, Bob drained the water into the slop sink. He set the table and poured water into two cups.

"Smells great," said the Old Man.

"Oh yeah..." said Bob, as he mounded pasta onto the two plates, and covered it with red sauce and meatballs.

The men ate in silence, enjoying each bite. When the Old Man's plate was empty, he pushed back from the table and tilted his head.

"Man, those are good meatballs, really hit the spot! And water gives life to the body," as he tipped back his cup. "You can really cook. It's good to have a partner who can swing an ax, but one that can cook is a rare find!"

"Thanks," said Bob Baker. "Grandma taught me to do both back in old Kentucky."

Bob cleared and cleaned the dishes in the slop sink. They lit a beeswax candle for light. Bob wrote in his journal while the Old Man nodded off, with his chin finally resting on his chest.

Bob's entry for December 16th read:

Missing Rae Ann and the kids but have a good gig, warm bunk, and hidden from hassles.

Illustration by Patrick Ruesch

4

TRAPLINE

The next morning, Bob awoke with a start to the Old Man and Lou moving around the one-room cabin. The past two years had made him a weary, light sleeper, always aware, watchful, and prepared for quick action. He slept more soundly in the little cabin than he had in a long time. The Old Man stirred the coals and added kindling and dry branches to the fire. The flames flickered to life and the chill receded from the room in a growing radius from the woodstove. Bob climbed down from the bunk and slid on his G. H. Bass leather moccasins.

"Morning," said the Old Man.

"Morning," Bob replied.

Coffee was percolating on the wood burner and a separate pot of water started to boil. They made oatmeal and added butter and brown sugar.

"OK, so let's talk a trapping plan," said the Old Man. They sat at the table, sipping the hot coffee. The Old Man pulled out a leather-bound notebook and showed Bob the shorthand record of how many traps he owned with what size and style they were. The next page had a list of locations for current sets. Toward the back of the book was a listing of different species of furbearers with the numbers he had caught this year.

"There are basically conibears, also called body grip traps, like this that dispatch the animals. They come in sizes 110, 220, or 330, along with other sizes for brands of traps that I don't use."

He showed Bob examples of each that he pulled out of a big wicker and leather pack.

"Then we also use some snares and footholds. These are the stakes, wires, trap chains, lures, nametags, and setting lever. I keep most equipment in these packs and plastic five-gallon buckets. We will load it onto the sleds and pull it behind the snowmobile."

"OK," said Bob Baker, as he inspected the metal springs and heavy-duty gear.

"I'll show you the skinning shed later when we go out," said the Old Man. "So right now, I've got 50 traps set. About 35 water sets for beaver and muskrat, over three different lakes. I've been seeing a lot more river otter as well. They thrive in clean waterways. There are 15 land sets for fisher, bobcat, pine martens, and coyotes in the woods," explained the Old Man.

"Wow, that's a lot!" said Bob.

"We'll be able to set more now that you are on board," said the Old Man with a wink. "The upland animals are just getting prime now, so we will shift some focus up there."

Bob's eyes bulged at the meticulously kept records.

"That's right," said the Old Man. "With this old brain, if I didn't write it down... I'd be littering metal all over Aroostook

County. Trapping has a very long history in these parts. The territory that is now Maine had several Native American tribes, including the Maliseet, Passamaquoddy, Abenaki, Micmac, and Penobscot. There were probably more small tribes that got pushed west into Canada early on. The Native peoples lived off the land and were true hunters and gatherers. They respected the land as a living thing and were part of that ecosystem and cycle. They made snares, fished and hunted, and lived with the land.

"Some of the early French explorers lived in harmony with the Natives. They intermarried and respected each other's ways. They were called the Acadians. When French and English trappers and traders arrived, it became a business. The Indians could trade pelts for metal goods, guns, and jewelry. What they didn't expect was disease and the constant influx of settlers. The Hudson's Bay Company had a presence here and exported a lot of pelts. By the late 1800s, northern Maine was over trapped. Wolves had been eradicated. That actually allowed white tailed deer to move north.

"In the 1940s, it was Clyde Wells of Saco and H.E. Ford of Berwick who were the big trappers. They started the Maine Trappers Association (MTA), and an emphasis was placed on conservation with seasons, limits, and regulations. The fur boom of the late 1970s and early 80s was when a fella could make some real cash on the trapline. People were quitting their day jobs and putting out steel in hopes of making a buck. In 1981, I saw two soccer moms fighting over a dead raccoon in the middle of a country road. Funny times. Past three decades, the number of trappers has steadily declined. Lot of factors I'm sure. Kids would rather play video games and watch tv and do organized sports. Folks are disconnected from Nature. Not much money in trapping, so that's not the motivation. I make enough to cover expenses and keep me and ol' Lou fed. But it's just me and this simple cabin. No mortgages, loans, or kids to fend for. You've got trade wars with Russia and China and a lot of ranched mink that drives fur prices down. You've got animal rights activists giving us a bad name, acting like animals are humans and saying we are inhumane. I care more about these animals than they will ever understand. I know this land and water on an intimate basis. I see the seasons change and become part of it. I study these animals' habits. Hunters, trappers, and fishermen are some of the stoutest proponents for conservation, preservation, and a land ethic.

"We see it as a gentle harvest. There is a certain carrying capacity to each microenvironment. Be it a pond, a lake, a section of woods, or a county. This is the maximum number of individuals of a given species that can live successfully on that habitat with those resources. Granted there are many factors, including other prey or predator species and weather. By trapping some animals, I see them replenish each year. I am careful to not over trap any particular area. I trap for the pleasure. The game of tricking the senses of beautiful creatures. A reason to be outside in Nature for extended periods of time. The thrill of checking traps.

"The biggest threat to trapping is climate change. That will likely do us all in, humans and every other creature on this planet spinning around in space. We cannot take, take, take and pollute with abandon and expect nothing to go wrong. We have to respect Nature and do all we can to protect the environment before it is too late. I mean..., look at Maine's state animal the moose. It is on our state flag for crying out loud. As the temperature has risen, there are more parasitic infections, and the moose herd is way down. I see a few, but not like I used to. I very seldom hunt them anymore, now I mostly just go after deer. We are all in this together. If more people trapped, I think they'd get a deeper understanding of the interconnectedness, and maybe work to preserve more."

"Wow! That was a semester of history, biology, and economics condensed into twenty minutes," said Bob.

"Yeah, I get pretty fired up about this stuff," quipped the Old Man. "Now let's get after it."

They packed a large thermos of coffee and two water bottles. Leftover meatballs were placed on fresh sour dough French bread and rolled in tinfoil. All of this was stashed into a leather satchel. The men layered on clothes: white long johns, sweatpants, jeans, and coveralls. Three layers on top as well. Scarves, wool hats, gloves, and large mitts over that. It was four degrees Fahrenheit and well below zero with the wind chill. The contrast was sharp and drastic between the cold, dry air outside and the comfortable cabin inside. The sun was shining and the breeze was slight, so the men were warm enough. Bob and the Old Man walked to the wooden barn about sixty feet from the cabin down a well-worn, stamped path through the snow. Inside the barn there were three beavers hanging from the rafters. Many other pelts were stretched on circular, wire structures. The Old Man showed Bob how to skin a beaver. He cut out portions of the thighs and back straps and placed them in a pot of water.

"These make for an excellent stew," said the Old Man. "The rest of the carcass we use for bait in the marten and coyote sets. There really isn't much waste. Commercial groups send the carcasses to a rendering plant. These here wooden boxes are for the martens."

The Old Man showed Bob a wooden box that looked like a rectangular bird house with no bottom.

"The bait goes in the top and the end is covered with a 110 or 220 conibear like this," said the Old Man, fitting in the trap. "Then it can be wired to a tree."

Once the beavers were skinned, the Old Man brought the meat pot into the cabin. Bob loaded the gear onto the thick rubber sled and hitched it to the snowmobile. Then they headed out down the line. They cruised along the trail and pulled down to a lake. The Old Man explained that they have a rotation to check each trap every other day. They chopped through the ice beside a large beaver lodge and pulled up the two sticks that were protruding through the ice.

"See how I have this stick through the rings of the conibear? I try to place it straight in the run where the beavers are leaving the lodge under the ice and swimming over there to their feed pile. You can see those bubble trails where they have been moving. Then this second stick stabilizes the trap jaws and prevents the beaver from swimming too far to that side."

Bob took it all in.

"This one is empty, but we will give it a few more days," said the Old Man.

They walked tentatively across the slick ice over to another lodge. Suddenly there came a sharp warbling, cracking sound that seemed to echo across the lake from where they stood. Bob crouched and threw out his arms in alarm.

"Whoa!" he yelled.

"Ha ha," chuckled the Old Man. "Don't worry, that's just the ice expanding," he said with a smile. "This ice is so thick you could drive a semi on it."

"Really?" asked Bob with a questioning frown. "It only seemed a few inches thick where we chopped through."

"Yeah, it's not as thick by the lodges because the critters' body heat and movements keep it thinner," said the Old Man.

"OK…" said Bob tentatively, "I just don't want to go swimmin'. We don't have ice like this in Kentucky."

"What brought you up here to the North Woods anyways?" asked the Old Man. "We aren't exactly a winter vacation destination."

The smile ran away from Bob's face, and he replied curtly, "It's been a rough couple of years for me, I'd rather not get into it."

Their eyes locked and the Old Man nodded understandingly, but his mind began to consider the scenarios. Maybe the sheriff was right? Was this irresponsible, being alone with an ex-convict? Would he regret it? Why was Bob so secretive? But then again, they had just met, and his character seemed quality.

They pulled a nice beaver out of the next trap and the Old Man showed Bob how to reset it. They did this with few words. The silence that had been so comfortable before now seemed strained. They finished checking and resetting the traps on that lake. Then they loaded the two beavers and one muskrat into a second rubber sled that was connected to the other sled with a two-foot length of chain. The brisk ride down the trail to the higher woods seemed to ease the tension between the two men.

"These rocky outcroppings with dense brush around are perfect for bobcat," said the Old Man.

"Why is that?" asked Bob.

"They often have dens in small caves for protection. There are a lot of rabbits and mice around, which make up a majority of their diet," explained the Old Man. "Bobcat numbers are up according to the DNR. We almost never see them because they are mostly nocturnal and very skittish. If you look in the right places, you'll find their signs though. Like here, that print in the snow is cat. The claws are retracted compared to this coyote trail over here with bigger pads and claw marks. You can tell the coyote stopped here to investigate the cat scent, then moved on his way. Bobcats will visit carrion piles for an easy meal, everything is just trying to survive the winter. Bobcats are susceptible to visual attractants, like feathers or fur, to get them to step on the trap. Coyotes rely more heavily on their noses."

"Interesting," said Bob.

They set five double spring foot traps for bobcats and coyotes, dabbing lures and baits in different sets.

"Wow, this is a beauty!" exclaimed the Old Man, as he pulled a prime, silky black marten from the opening of a wooden box attached to the trunk of a white pine.

"Sure is," Bob said as he stroked the fine animal and bungee strapped it into the sled with the beavers and muskrat.

They drove the snow machine along the trail a few

hundred yards, parked it, and walked the equipment into the woods to make the sets. They brought any trapped animals back to the sled. One set held an angry coyote. He was a big male, caught by a front left paw. As the men approached, the coyote pulled back as far as the trap chain would allow. He snarled and bared his yellowish canines. The Old Man dug down through his layers of clothes and pulled an old .22 pistol from the holster on his belt. The shot broke the silence of the woods and the animal dropped. Bob pulled the coyote over to the sled and the Old Man reset the trap, explaining that the scent of this animal will attract others. By now it was late afternoon, and the men were hungry. They pulled alongside the trail at a curve and shut off the engine.

"I often stop here for lunch," said the Old Man. "These two trees tipped over across the trail a couple years ago. I cut them up for wood, but the stumps make for table and chairs."

They poured hot black coffee from the thermos into their two metal cups.

"Good stuff," said Bob. "This trapping is not easy. Rough on the hands and back, lifting, pulling, squeezing."

"No joke. I'm sure there are easier ways to make a buck, but I enjoy being my own boss, living off the land, and this sure beats an office or a factory," he said, waving his hand at the surroundings.

"No doubt," agreed Bob, as he unwrapped the sandwiches from the tinfoil.

The meatballs and sauce were still slightly warm, and the condensation had softened the bread to perfection.

They finished lunch and headed back down the trail on the snowmobile.

"Our last stop is Lake Marie," said the Old Man. "Then we head back."

The sun was fading on the western horizon when they got back to the woodshed to hang up the catch. Gear organized and stowed, they got back in the cabin and stoked the fire. Bob grilled marinated venison backstraps with onions on the woodstove and they ate. Then the Old Man went to the cabinet and pulled out a bottle of Kentucky bourbon.

"I thought this would make you feel at home," he said, as he showed the bottle to Bob.

"Heck yeah," said Bob appreciatively.

The Old Man poured the alcohol into two glasses over ice and handed one across the wooden table.

"Cheers to a good day on the trapline."

Bob's journal entry for December 17th read:

Trapping is an interesting endeavor. I've never seen so much snow and ice. This landscape is very different from the green hills of Kentucky but has a beauty all its own. The Old Man's knowledge, strength, and determination are impressive. He's curious why I'm here, can't say that I blame him.

5

DEATH ON THE TRAIL

The trapping was going very well, and the Old Man was pleased with the amount of prime furs that had piled up in the shed. The regional fur buyer was coming to Allagash and the Old Man was going to take the pelts in for the sale.

"OK," the Old Man said to Bob, "here's the plan. I'm going to load up the sled and take Lou with me into town to sell these furs. You can go up in the hills and try to shoot a deer because our venison supply is getting low."

"Sounds good to me," said Bob enthusiastically.

Once the sled was loaded down with furs, the two men shook hands and parted ways. Bob loaded his rifle and headed for the pine woods where he had seen a lot of deer sign while trapping. He could hear the hum of the Old Man's snowmobile slowly disappearing toward Allagash.

It was a beautiful morning. The sun was shining and the fresh inch of powder sparkled like thousands of shimmering prisms scattered on the ground. The air was cold and crisp, but the sun made it very pleasant. Bob Baker was wearing sunglasses to prevent the snow burn to his retinas, which many skiers and outdoorsmen warn about.

Photograph by Patrick Ruesch

As he made his way into the pines, he was thinking about how happy he was with this trapping arrangement and the Old Man himself. Bob's dad died in a coal mining accident when Bob was just ten. Although he had a very strong, supportive mom, siblings, and extended family, he had longed for a father figure. The Old Man was a pleasure to learn from and live with.

Bob's mind was quickly brought back to the task at hand as he saw movement up ahead in a thick patch of brush. This area of rolling foothills was covered with mature white pines and Douglas fir. There were areas that had been logged within the past twenty years, and these were overgrown with brushy, deciduous trees. Bob was already anticipating the end of the hunt, which would be ideal if it ended this close to home.

Bob noticed some movement up ahead again and was able to pick out wide forked antlers moving beside a white pine trunk. His boots moved silently in the powdery snow. As he stepped around the edge of a tree, he saw a nice mature buck standing broadside at fifty yards. He slowly raised his rifle, aimed behind the front shoulder, held his breath, and carefully squeezed the trigger. The split second before the .308 fired, a crow cawed angrily at Bob Baker, the intruder. The wise deer flinched and ducked at the sudden sound of the upset bird. The carefully placed shot ended up high and forward on the deer, smashing through the shoulder blade and through the muscle on the far side. The deer felt the searing hot sting of metal as it hightailed it farther into the woods.

"Shoot!" Bob exclaimed. "Dang it," he said. "Darn crow."

He waited fifteen minutes before pursuing the deer, as sometimes that can give the animal a chance to weaken and die even after a misplaced shot. Bob then approached the deer's location and found bright red blood splattered on the white snow. The deer's tracks and blood were easy to follow. Bob trailed the deer for two hours, which was not easy through the knee-high snow. By then the amount of blood on the trail was slowing.

The deer's tracks were getting closer together, meaning he was just as tired as Bob Baker.

The deer led him through a briar thicket, the edge of a swamp, and through an overgrown tangle of fallen, burned snags from a forest fire many decades before. By now it was afternoon and Bob wished he had packed a lunch. He thought the hunt would be quick and he'd have time to wait for the Old Man.

Meanwhile, the Old Man was in town at the fur sale.

"Hey hey there, old timer," said Dean, the fur buyer from Portland. "That's quite a pile of fur you got there."

"Ayup, I'm happy with it," said the Old Man with a smile.

"He's got help with him out on the trapline this year," said Ted Thompson.

"Oh yeah, who's that?" asked Dean.

"He's got an *ex-con* working with him," said Ted disdainfully.

"I don't care what he was in the past," said the Old Man. "He's a heck of a reliable worker and great company."

"So, you left him out at the cabin alone while you're here?" asked Dean with a persecutory frown. "He's probably robbing you blind!"

"What's he going to take from my cabin? Anyhow, he's just not that kind of guy," said the Old Man.

"Well, you're gonna be getting top dollar for these furs anyways," said Dean as he looked through the carefully skinned pelts. "Lot of nice animals here. Now be careful with this ex-convict character. I wouldn't trust him, especially with all this cash on hand."

"I'll take care of myself," said the Old Man with a sharp glance, as he put the money into his pocket.

Bob Baker sat on a tree stump and shook his head. *This is a tough old deer*, he thought to himself with a half-smile. He's leading me through the roughest ground in the North Woods just to get back at me for what I did to him. Bob had to admire the strength and determination to survive that this old buck possessed. He felt bad that the animal was wounded and he did not want to give up the chase - he knew it would be a waste of meat and more suffering for the deer. With these thoughts in mind, he kept on the trail.

At one point, Bob found a spot where the deer had bedded down in some thick cattails. There was a pile of blood in the melted snow. This gave him confidence that the deer was weakening. The sun was setting and Bob was afraid nightfall would make the trail too difficult to follow. Just then he crested a small hill and looked down the gentle valley below. He could see the deer walking head down, plodding through the snow. Bob rested his rifle on the low branch of a tree and steadied the open sights on the slow-moving animal. It was at least 150 yards, but he felt confident in the old rifle and knew this may be his only chance to bring down the deer. He held his breath and pulled the trigger. The report of the rifle echoed down the valley and the deer stumbled and fell. Bob exhaled a huge cloud of frozen mist, *whooo*, and breathed a sigh of relief.

The Old Man returned to the cabin with an empty sled, leaping heart, and full wallet. This was the best sale of fur he had in many years. He loved to see the admiration on the other trappers' faces. And to think, they had told him to quit trapping and move to town years ago. When he got back to the cabin, he was surprised to find it empty.

"What in the world?" said the Old Man. "Where did that guy get off to?"

He looked around but there was no note, and the coals in the fire were getting cold.

"Huh," he said, with a bit of worry coming to his voice.

It was now dark outside and the Old Man knew all too well what a twisted ankle or a broken leg can lead to in the frigid North Woods. He checked the fur shed and then fired up the snowmobile.

By the time Bob had walked to the fallen deer, the last rays of sunlight were gone. He squatted down and pet the large animal and said some words of thanksgiving to the cycle of Nature that had allowed their paths to cross. He pulled his skinning knife from the sheath on his belt and gutted the large deer. As he grabbed the back two legs and started to drag the deer, he realized this was an impossible task. He was bone-tired, had not eaten anything since breakfast, and he was fifteen miles from the cabin, across uneven ground with two feet of snow. The last thing he wanted was for the coyotes to eat his bounty of venison, but there was no way he was packing that deer out tonight.

He took a rope from his pack and put it through the leg tendons on the big buck. He threw the end of the rope over a large oak branch and pulled the deer off the ground. It was no easy task as the rope pinched on the branch under the weight of the big deer. He then tied the rope off to the trunk of the tree and started for the cabin.

The Old Man and Lou found Bob's tracks leading up to the pine woods where they had trapped marten the month before. The Old Man could read sign better than he could read books, and he quickly found the spot where the deer was first shot.

"Where could he be?" said the Old Man to the dog.

The dog lifted his eyebrows and barked once, as if to say, "How should I know what you crazy humans do?"

The Old Man was worried that his trapping partner and friend could be curled up and frozen. He tried to go as quickly as he could on the snowmobile but then would get off track. The Old Man could hear coyotes barking and yipping in the distance. Occasionally Lou would let out a low howl as if his wild cousins were still family.

After he drove five miles on the trail, he suddenly saw movement in the headlights. It was Bob Baker walking head down, somewhat in the direction of the cabin.

"Boy am I glad to see you, old timer," Bob Baker said in a tired voice.

"Man, I was worried about you Bob," said the Old Man as he stopped the snowmobile. He ran up and gave Bob a hug and then a pat on the shoulder as if to hide his worry.

Bob explained what had happened with the deer and pointed down the low valley.

"Well geez," said the Old Man. "Most people would've left that deer for the coyotes hours ago. You've gotta be starved."

"I wasn't gonna let him suffer just because I can't shoot straight," said Bob with an exhausted smile.

The Old Man said, "Let's get that deer and get back to the cabin," as they climbed on the snow machine and headed downhill.

As they were approaching the hanging deer, they could see four coyotes who had already picked over the gut pile and were jumping up at the swinging deer carcass.

"Dern yotes," said the Old Man as he stopped the snowmobile.

Bob and the Old Man loaded their rifles and aimed over the hood of the snowmobile. The full moon on the fresh snow made everything visible.

"You take the one on the right, I got the one on the left," said the Old Man. "On the count of three. One, two, three."

The two rifles sounded like one as the percussion split the night. The two coyotes spun and fell into a permanent sleep in the snow. The other two took off at a dead run toward the woods. Both rifles fired again at the retreating coyotes, but all they hit was snow.

They loaded the deer and the two dead coyotes onto the sled and tied them down. The Old Man hit the gas and headed for home. They hung the deer and the coyotes in the fur shed and went inside for food. Bob Baker took a warm bath while the Old Man got dinner ready. It was fresh venison steaks, sautéed with minced garlic, onions, mushrooms, and soy sauce, along with biscuits prepared with garlic salt, butter, and shredded cheddar cheese mixed into the batter. By the time Bob got out of the bath and slumped into the wooden chair by the table, the food was ready. He wasn't sure which was more severe, the hunger or the exhaustion. He cleared his plate as the Old Man started to tell him how much money they made on the furs. Bob Baker didn't hear a word. He was making his way up the ladder to the bunk and was asleep as soon as his head hit the pillow.

As Bob was snoring softly, the Old Man took out his journal and began to write:

January 17th

Folks in town are concerned about my choice of a hired hand. Bob has carried his weight each day and showed true character in finishing the hunt today. Everyone deserves a second chance. And I'm sure enjoying the company and help.

6

END OF THE LINE

The trapping season continued to go well until the end of February, when the weather was getting unseasonably warm and the pelts were past their peak. They had pulled all the traps except the ones on Lake Marie. There were ten conibear sets at the lake. Three large 330s were set at each of two different beaver lodges along the east shore, and four smaller 110s set near some muskrat bank dens on the opposite shore. The trail was close to the south shore, so the men parked there.

"I'll go pull the beaver sets," said the Old Man. "You get the muskrat ones, and we'll meet back at the sled."

They each took their axes and walked out across the slushy ice. Since the weather had warmed, they switched from heavy 2,000 grain boots to insulated, waterproof muck boots. Bob got to the muskrat sets and chopped out two of the four traps, both empty. As he approached the third set, he glanced out across the lake expanse but didn't see the Old Man. Bob was surprised and looked closer. Then he noticed a bobbing, dark object just above the ice.

"Oh shingles!" he yelled.

Photograph by John Plescia

Panic was the first feeling, but he calmed his emotions and thought it out, speaking to himself to get a plan. The distance to the Old Man or to the snowmobile was about equal, at 250 yards either way. Unfortunately, the safety rope was at the sled and Bob knew without that they'd probably both end up drowned. He dropped all his gear and ran splashing across the wet ice to the snowmobile. Breathless, he started the engine and motored through the slush and brush at the edge of Lake Marie, headed for the Old Man. Bob didn't want to risk driving the heavy snow machine onto the thin ice. He got as close to the Old Man as he could and left the snowmobile on the shore.

Bob tied the 100-foot nylon rope to a birch tree, and holding the one-foot wooden stake at the opposite end, ran onto the ice. The Old Man was nowhere to be seen. Then his head rose out of the water like a turtle gasping at the center of the opening. It was obvious that he'd broken through and repeatedly tried to crawl out on top of the ice. The edges were too thin and he kept breaking through, enlarging the watery circle. His strength waned, and now only his face, and occasionally an outstretched hand, rose above the water and ice chunks.

"Help!" the Old Man gasped, as his head rose again like a fish mouthing the surface in an oxygen-starved pool of drought water.

"Hang on!" yelled Bob.

He knew the Old Man was in no shape to grab and hold the tow stick, so he tied the rope around his own waist and ran full tilt toward his drowning partner. When Bob was five feet from the Old Man the ice gave way under Bob's boots and he pitched forward into the icy water. The shock of the frigid water was even more than he had expected, and it took his breath away. Adrenaline was coursing through his vessels and the ancient fight or flight response, innate to all creatures, was driving him on. Bob doggie paddled past chunks of ice to where the Old Man last floated, but he was gone. Bob looked around the watery grave but couldn't find his friend. He felt something brush his elbow. It could have been one of the numerous floating ice chunks in the water, but it felt softer, with more give. Just then Bob saw the Old Man's black and red checkered hat and reached down to grab his limp body. His pale face was blue at the lips, no breathing.

"Hang on old timer!" Bob yelled, as he looped his left arm under the man's armpits.

Bob tried to grip the rope with his gloved hand, but there was no function. His wet gloves were too bulky, he had water in his eyes, and couldn't get positioned. He shook the wet gloves off, wiped his face and gripped the rope with his bare right hand, all the while treading with his legs. He pulled himself and the dead weight of the Old Man across the small watery opening to the ice's edge. The ice kept breaking as Bob tried to slide the Old Man on top of it. He broke a small path until they got to thicker ice, away from the beaver lodge. Eventually he was able to slide the Old Man onto the ice and crawl out himself.

Bob dragged the Old Man to shore. Their wet clothes were stiffening in the cold air. The Old Man still was not breathing and there was no radial pulse at the wrist. Bob started CPR with chest compressions. After just two or three deep presses on the sternum, the Old Man started to cough and sputter. Lake water splattered out of his mouth into the ice crystals that had formed in his beard. He was mumbling and the deep blue in his lips was fading. The carotid pulse in his neck picked up as he continued to cough and clear his airway.

"Let's get out of here," Bob chattered.

He dragged the Old Man up the bank, through some brush, to the snowmobile. He untied the rope from his waist and started the engine.

Thank heavens it started, Bob thought, *or we'd freeze to death right here.*

Bob strapped the Old Man on the seat in front of him and maneuvered the snowmobile through the brush back to the main trail. It was slow going in the thick snow and shrubby trees. He didn't want to move too quickly and tip over with the unconscious man sitting limp. Finally, they got back to the main trail and could give it gas. Bob's right hand was painfully cold with no glove, so he jammed it into his pocket for a while before switching repeatedly with his left hand. His wet clothes had completely hardened into a frozen exoskeleton. Any exposed skin burned. His eyelashes were sheets of ice and wouldn't allow his eyes to fully close. It was a painful ride back to the cabin. They sped into the yard and jammed on the brakes, skidding to a stop. Bob was half frozen to the Old Man and the seat of the snowmobile. He could feel his energy draining as he dragged the Old Man up the steps and pushed open the door.

Bob pulled the Old Man to the middle of the room and they both collapsed on the floor. Lou barked excitedly and licked at his master's face, unsure about this unusual entrance. There were hot coals in the wood stove but no flames. Bob got to his feet as the iron shell of his clothes started to thaw. He shut the door to the air outside and let the 50-degrees of the cabin wash over him and fill his chilled lungs. He put kindling on the fire and started pulling off the Old Man's layered clothes. He was coughing and moaning while Lou paced and jumped around the room nervously. Finally, Bob got him down to just underwear. His feet and hands were cold and blue, but his core was warm. Bob dried him with towels and wrapped him in a wool Indian blanket. Then Bob folded the Old Man into an open sleeping bag laid out in front of the woodstove.

He put birch logs onto the crackling fire and stripped off his own wet clothes. He placed the kettle full of water on the stovetop and readied two mugs for tea. Lou curled up next to his owner. After an hour, the Old Man's mumbling was more coherent, and he opened his eyes. Bob fed him spoonfuls of black tea with honey.

"Did we make it?" the Old Man asked in a whisper.

"Yeah we did, but not by much," answered Bob.

They sipped tea and fell into a deep slumber, with the cabin warming to 65 degrees and easing their exhausted bodies back to baseline.

7

FEAR OF THE UNKNOWN

The next day the Old Man slowly regained his strength. "A chilling like that can be the end of an old timer like me," he said. "You really saved my bacon out there. Much longer in that ice water and I would've been a goner. And even if I did get out, no way I'd have made it back to the cabin."

"Well maybe you saved me too," said Bob, "by letting me come out here and trap with you. Not many folks would've taken in a stranger, especially with all the rumors swirling around town. If I didn't get out of Muhlenberg County, I could be back in prison or worse."

"Happy to have you Bob." The Old Man was curious and considered asking for more details but hesitated due to the wall of resistance Bob had put up earlier in the trapping season. He decided to respect Bob's privacy and leave it at that.

"I don't know your past Bob, and I don't need to. From what I see, you are a good man. Trust your instincts, work hard, do right by people, and things should work out fine," said the Old Man.

"Thanks", said Bob sincerely.

Photograph by John Plescia

Over the next few days, they rested and worked on skinning the last catches of the year. They also cleaned and stored the trapping equipment. It was sunny and a little warmer.

"It is important to take good care of your supplies when working a long trapline in the north country," said the Old Man. "The cold and snow are tough on the moving parts of traps, snowmobiles, buildings, and the people that work in these rural places."

When most of the end-of-season work was done, the Old Man asked Bob about his plans.

"Well," said Bob, "I've fallen in love with this country and I'd sure like to get my family up here to experience it. The kids will be on summer break soon."

"There's a camp just north of here called Camp Okimachobee where they have troubled kids come out from Portland. I know the owner, name is Mitch Cedar. He's a great guy and often is looking for help. I could put in a word."

"That sounds good, thanks," said Bob.

"As the weather warms up in the next few weeks, I have a guy coming from California with a semi full of beehives," continued the Old Man.

"What are you having beehives brought up here for?" asked Bob.

"There's been a shortage of wild honeybees due to colony collapse syndrome and we need bees to pollinate all the trees, and my garden," he said with a wink. "And besides, they're going to pay me twenty-five percent of their honey proceeds just for keeping their hives out here. It won't be much work for me, *and* I can use the extra money," he said with another wink.

"Wow, nice," said Bob. "I'll head into town to write a letter to Rae Ann and the kids to see if they're interested in coming up here for the summer."

"Ayup, I'll go pay Mitch a visit and see if he can use your help at the camp," said the Old Man.

The past few days of hanging around the cabin and working in the barn had left Bob itching to get out into the fresh air and do some hiking. He left the Old Man cleaning the windows of the cabin and walked ten miles into town. The temperature had been climbing into the forties during the day, making the snow slushy and the creeks starting to rise. The wild North Woods had truly grown on Bob Baker, and the thought of leaving the Old Man really made Bob want to stay for the summer. He also missed Rae Ann, Claire, and Henry and hoped they'd get excited about coming up. When Bob got out of prison, the circumstances that got him in there in the first place had not changed much. Muhlenberg County, Kentucky was still corrupt, and rumor had it that the Lewis brothers were still looking to even the score. But Bob's mind was clear as he walked down the wooded trail with the optimism of spring all around him.

He made it into town and went in Two Rivers Lunch.

"Hi Emma," said Bob with a quick wave.

"Hey Bob, sit anywhere you'd like," said the young waitress with a smile.

Bob noticed Sheriff Ted Thompson sitting with two other gray-haired men along the back wall. They all looked up when Bob entered but then went back to their meals. Bob took off his coat and hat and laid them on the neighboring seat. Emma came over with coffee and took his order. As he was talking to her, he caught the words "prison" and "old man" coming from the sheriff's booth. The rest of the discussion was too low for him to understand. Occasionally one of the old men would glance his way while they were talking.

Bob took out his notebook and started writing while sipping the black coffee.

Dear Rae Ann,

I hope this note finds you in good health and spirits. Spring has come to the North Woods and I miss ya'll like crazy. Like I have said before, the Old Man I've been trapping with is super cool. He has a nice old dog named Lou that the kids would really like. We did well trapping. I learned a lot and saw some beautiful country.

How are things there? Any word from Uncle Tommy? Have you seen the Lewis crowd anywhere?

I have an idea for the summer. There is a camp here for kids that have behavioral problems. They come from the city and spend a lot of time doing activities outside. The owner of the camp may have a job for us to help out there. I know Henry would miss baseball and Claire would miss swimming, but I think they'd have fun up here too. It's not for sure yet, but I should hear from the camp owner soon. Let me know what you think. Would probably be good for you to get out of Kentucky for the summer.

Tell the kids I love them and can't wait to see them again.

Lots of love,
Bob

While he was writing Emma brought over his corn beef and hash. The two old men who Bob did not recognize put on their coats and walked to the door, giving Bob dirty looks as they passed. A couple of minutes later Ted Thompson left his tip on the table where their empty plates sat and walked over to Bob.

"Listen here," said Ted with a no-nonsense look on his face. "I don't know who you are or what you're up to, but I strongly suggest you pack up and head out. That Old Man is one of us, we won't stand for some out-of-towner takin' advantage of him."

The sheriff's palms were flat on the table and he seemed extremely large, looking down on Bob who was seated and finishing his meal. Bob could feel his blood starting to boil, and the hairs on his neck rise.

"If you don't know me, why do you assume I'm a danger to the Old Man or anyone else? Is it because of rumors you've heard?" Bob said, as he raised his eyes to meet the sheriff's.

"No more talk," said Ted Thompson in a low growl. "If you know what's good for you, you'll clear out." With that he turned and headed out the door.

Bob's blood pressure started to come down.

Emma frowned at Bob from behind the counter. "Sorry Bob. He's just stubborn and stuck in his ways, not real open to new ideas or people. He's not a bad man, he really does care about keeping everyone safe," said Emma apologetically. "He's a true Moosetowner," she added.

"What does that mean?" asked Bob frowning.

"It means Sherriff Thompson was born and raised here, and it has not always been easy. The population of Allagash has plummeted over the years. Not many good jobs, people just pack up and leave, go south to bigger towns. Sure, there are some timber jobs with Irving forestry and outdoor guiding services, but otherwise, not much opportunity. Some residents feel it is 'us against them.' We are out here on the edge of nothing, end of the road, they don't understand how other people think or feel. Ted Thompson has never left here for any length of time. He's skeptical and suspicious of you because of your accent and newness."

Bob nodded and said, "Good hash."

He considered changing the letter to his wife, or even crumpling it into a ball and throwing it away. Instead he folded it in three, placed it in the envelope, and put the address and stamp on it.

Back at the cabin, the Old Man was getting the windows as clear as the water on Lake Marie. With the sun shining on his back, he too felt the optimism of spring and hoped that Bob would stick around. Maybe he'd get to meet the Baker family. He walked to his red pickup with Lou at his heels, started the engine, and drove to Camp Okimachobee to find Mitch.

Photograph by Trisha Plescia

8

DRONES

The plentiful sunshine and warmer weather had melted off most of the snow, so the Old Man could drive his truck over to Camp Okimachobee and talk to Mitch Cedar.

"Hey there old timer," said Mitch, as the red Chevy door opened and the Old Man climbed out stiffly.

"Made it through another winter," said the Old Man.

"Hallelujah," said Mitch. "What's going on?"

"I've got a friend looking for work, and I thought maybe he could help you out with the camp this year. He's a hard worker and a smart guy. I spent all winter trapping with him. Name's Bob Baker. He's got a wife and two kids. A boy who's nine and a daughter who's twelve, and they're all thinking about coming here for the summer."

"Yeah, I could use the help. As long as they don't mind staying in the camp house," said Mitch.

"Shouldn't be a problem," said the Old Man. "I'll let him know."

That evening, the Old Man relayed the good news to Bob. After dinner Bob wrote a letter to his family explaining that the summer camp job prospect was confirmed, and he put it in the mail the next day.

The only snow remaining was that which was hiding in the shadows of the big pines and firs. Bob Baker and the Old Man were splitting firewood behind the cabin when they heard a distant rumble of a large truck. The sound slowly got closer and the Old Man said that it was probably the delivery of the beehives. Sure enough, a large white eighteen-wheel semi came up the soft roadbed, gouging deep ruts. It pulled carelessly into the side yard and put on the brakes.

The man that climbed out of the driver's seat wore a dirty red baseball cap with greasy, grayish-brown hair sticking out from the sides. Bob Baker and the Old Man came around the side of the house to greet these beekeepers. The man that came out of the passenger side was tall and skinny, with a pointed nose and a thin black goatee that gave him the look of a weasel. As they got closer, they could see the man with the dirty red hat had only one good eye. His left eye looked like a milk-colored marble and his good eye would never look straight at you.

"Name's One-Eyed-Joe. We got the bees," the man said abruptly. His handshake was limp and his odor was offensive.

"I'm Slim, heh heh heh," wheezed the skinny man.

Suddenly, the back of the trailer opened and two more men jumped out.

"Wow, quite a crew you have," said the Old Man.

"These here are Mack and Joyce," said One-Eyed-Joe.

Bob Baker did not like the feel of this group from the beginning. Neither did the Old Man, but he figured he wouldn't have to deal with these people very much. They would set up the beehives, occasionally add boxes, and then take them away in the early fall.

"Where are these hives going?" asked One-Eyed-Joe curtly.

"Right around here," said the Old Man as he showed them behind the barn.

"Wow, you guys split all that wood by hand, huh?" said Joe. "Slim here can barely pick up an ax."

"Heh heh heh," said Slim as he spit tobacco juice all over the ground, half of it dribbling into his goatee. When he laughed his rotten teeth shook like dry aspen leaves in the fall.

Bob Baker and the Old Man showed the beekeepers the clearing behind the cabin where the grass was just changing from brown to light green.

"Yeah, this'll do fine," muttered Joe as he yelled at Mack and Joyce to start unloading the equipment.

First, they put down wooden pallets in a long row on the north side of the clearing. Then they unloaded white hive bodies and set the boxes two in a stack, with four stacks on each pallet. The men all worked up a sweat after a few trips back and forth from the semi. One-Eyed-Joe did a lot more barking orders than actually moving equipment. Lou, who normally liked strangers and typically would be running around playing in the grass, sat on the edge of the porch watching the activity and occasionally letting out a low snarl.

The Old Man and Bob noticed this and gave each other a sideways glance. Once all the boxes were in place, One-Eyed-Joe instructed everyone to pry out the small wooden spacers from the opening of the hives and insert a plastic feeder that was full of cherry Kool-Aid. The bees started moving in and out of the hives, exploring the new surroundings. The work was done, and the men were standing in a circle.

Mack fondled his black ponytail and said, "So Slim, what is this Old Man cooking us for lunch?"

"Heh heh heh, better be beer and steaks," said Slim.

The Old Man announced that they only had some leftover chicken soup and water. He wasn't expecting such a big group but they were welcome to share the food.

"No, forget it," said One-Eyed-Joe. "We're headed into town."

Bob Baker noticed the California license plates on the semi and asked Joe where they got all the beehives.

Joe squinted and his one good eye tried to focus on Bob but seemed to dip toward the ground. "Not that it's any of your business," said Joe coldly, "but we get the hives from the desert southwest where they raise queens. We'll be back in a couple weeks to check on things."

Mack and Joyce jumped into the trailer and slammed the doors, like two monkeys putting themselves in a cage. Slim slithered into the passenger seat and rolled down the window to spit a brown stream. The semi rolled out of the drive and the big ruts filled with water.

Bob Baker said to the Old Man, "That's a shady bunch if I ever did see one."

"No doubt," said the old timer. "Let's go eat."

9

CAMP OKIMACHOBEE

Bob Baker got a letter back from his family that said they were all in for coming to Maine that summer. The plan was for them to leave Kentucky as soon as school got out the first week of June. Bob immediately told the Old Man the good news. They headed over to see Mitch Cedar at Camp Okimachobee. Mitch was happy that the arrangement was set.

"Well Bob, no reason to waste time. If you're ready, I can show you around the camp," said Mitch. Bob and the Old Man followed Mitch around the campgrounds. It was difficult to estimate Mitch's age. He had a full head of thick gray hair, large strong hands, and a tan clean-shaved face. Deep crow's feet lined the corners of his eyes when he smiled, which was often. He lacked the typical belly of a man in his late fifties. He wore a blue checkered flannel shirt tucked into Wrangler jeans. His back was straight, but he carried a mild limp when walking too quickly.

"Here is the camp bunk house where the students will sleep. Here is the side room for you and your family. There is one bathroom for everyone to share."

Then Bob said, "So what are the requirements for kids to come here? Do they have educational problems, or behavioral problems, or do they just like to camp?"

"Well," said Mitch, "it is an intercity program that takes kids with behavioral problems at school or home and brings them out to Nature to help expose them to the great outdoors and hopefully improve their disposition. A lot of them have given their parents and teachers all kinds of hassles and we try to help them out."

"Sounds interesting," said Bob, "and challenging."

Next Mitch led Bob down to the boathouse. He unlocked the padlock and opened the big wooden door. There were eight canoes and two kayaks stacked on one side and life jackets, paddles, and fishing poles on the other. There was plenty of dust and cobwebs from the long winter break.

"This can be your first project," said Mitch, "after I'm done giving you a tour of the place. You can dust off all the equipment and get it ready for the season."

The two men walked down by Kyte Creek, which was swollen with melted snow and ice from the surrounding hills. The water was clear and cold with several small ice jams floating downstream.

"Plenty of trout in this stream and lots of good canoeing for the campers," said Mitch.

They hiked up through the surrounding spruce and pine flats and circled back to the camp. Mitch showed Bob one last shed that had big plastic containers with many tents, coffee pots, and camping gear.

"The students will arrive in one month," said Mitch.

"Oh perfect," said Bob. "That's when my family will arrive as well."

The weeks passed quickly as everyone was busy preparing for the campers to arrive. The Bakers came in Bob's old green Ford pickup truck on the first Saturday of June. The truck was more rust than paint. Rae Ann got out of the driver's side door while Claire and Henry jumped out of the passenger side.

"You made it!" cried Bob. He ran over and wrapped them all in a tight bear hug, shocked at how much taller and older his children were.

They all felt like laughing and crying simultaneously and held onto each other for a long while. "We missed you so much!" Rae Ann gave Bob a kiss on the lips.

"What has mama been feeding you guys?!" he exclaimed.

Henry chuckled as he pulled a big brown paper bag full of foul-smelling greenery out of the truck. "She's been feeding us tons of swiss chard from the garden... I wanted to remind you of home so brought you some!"

"Oh... so thoughtful of you!" said Bob sarcastically, grimacing and wrestling his son to the ground.

The family chatted a while longer, catching up on the past months. Then Bob grabbed Rae Ann's hand and said, "Well, let me show you around Camp Okimachobee. Over here is the lodge. You can see all the bunk beds for the campers, who will be arriving tomorrow. And here is our room, with three beds and an attached bathroom. Here is the big cafeteria where we'll be cooking and eating. But the best part of this whole camp is the outdoors."

"Dad, you said in your letter that there was a creek we could canoe in?" asked Henry.

"Absolutely!" said Bob. "Kyte Creek, and it runs right over here through the woods. It's a great trout stream and spot to canoe. Let's get your luggage unpacked and then we'll take the canoe out."

"It feels good to stretch our legs," said Rae Ann. "It's a long road from Kentucky."

The family was thrilled to be back together and brought all the luggage from the truck into their room. When that was done and things were organized, they headed to the storage shed and pulled out a 16-foot, green fiberglass Old Town canoe. They all put life jackets on and tucked a tackle box, four fishing poles, and a Styrofoam cup full of worms into the canoe. They pushed the front of the canoe into the water. Rae Ann climbed in and sat down in the front seat, and then Claire and Henry behind her. Bob pushed the canoe the rest of the way into the water and hopped in. The children sat on wooden handrails as they navigated down the clear water of Kyte Creek. Some of the turns held fallen trees from the winter freeze and the spring melt.

"You have to be careful of these strainers," said Bob, pointing at the tangles of branches. "Especially in the faster water."

"The air is so fresh up here," commented Claire.

"Sure is," said Bob. "This is going to be a fun summer! The nice thing about canoeing is that lakes, streams, and rivers are always a little different every time you are on them. Just think, there can be fallen trees, more or less water, cold and clear, or warm and muddy. The wind is never the same, the plants and animals are always changing, and we feel different on each day. It is an adventure anew each time."

The next curve held a slow-moving deep spot that Bob called a hole. He ruddered the canoe off to the shallow side and they all climbed out onto the rocky shore. They untangled the poles and put worms on the hooks.

"Now cast up there at the start of the deep spot, and let the worms float down," Bob encouraged.

Claire was the first to cast and almost as soon as the worm hit the moving water, she felt a tug. "Wow!" she yelled, and yanked the line. "Fish on fish on!" she whooped.

"Reel it in, quick!" called Henry.

As she pulled in the line, they saw a glimmering fish move through the water and jump out above the ripples. She got it up to shore. They could see it was a beautiful brook trout.

"Sweet!" said Bob. "That's a nice fish. He's a keeper for sure."

He tucked a piece of nylon rope through the fish's mouth and out the gills. He fastened it to the canoe and let the fish swim in the water.

The next few casts didn't connect with any fish. But then Henry gave a tug on his line and said, "I got one, I got one! It feels like a monster!"

But as he reeled it toward shore, Bob could tell the line was not moving except for his son pulling it. As he pulled his line out of the water, they could see a two-foot-long maple branch with mud and leaves connected to it.

"Oh pooch," said Henry.

"That's called a stick fish," said Rae Ann, smiling and ruffling his thick brown hair, "and it's a keeper just for you Henry."

Over the next twenty minutes, Rae Ann, Bob, and Henry each caught fish. Bob's was a creek chub, which he quickly released. Rae Ann's was a small brook trout with speckled markings on its sides, but it was too small to keep. Henry's first fish of the summer was a fourteen-inch, meaty brook trout. They added it to the stringer and continued downstream.

"What a great little fishing spot that was," said Bob. "But we've got to keep moving. We have somebody to meet at the other end."

For the next two hours they paddled through beautiful spruce hills and wet meadows. The twenty-foot wide Kyte Creek was flowing nicely with winter runoff. Finally, they approached an overpass and Bob steered the canoe toward the right bank. They could see a faint wisp of campfire smoke as they pulled up on shore. The Old Man was tending to the coals and had four folding camp chairs and a card table set up.

"Hey there old timer!" Bob yelled as they pulled the canoe up on shore. "Here's my family! This is Rae Ann, Claire, and Henry."

"It's my lucky day," said the Old Man. "I've enjoyed the company of one Baker, and now I get the pleasure of meeting three more."

"Bob sure has learned a lot from you over the winter," said Rae Ann. She reached for his hand with both of hers.

"You're a real live woodsman, aren't you?" asked Henry, raising his eyebrows and bouncing from foot to foot.

"We heard you have a nice dog named Lou," said Claire. "Where is he?"

"Oh, he's resting in the back of the truck. You can go let him out if you want."

The two kids raced up the gravel turnoff to meet the dog. Bob cleaned the two trout and tossed the guts into the bushes for the coons. He rinsed off the fish and put them in tin foil with lemon and onion slices, salt, pepper, and butter. He sealed the tin foil and dropped them into the hot coals. The Old Man and Rae Ann sat in camp chairs, eating peanuts from the shell and talking.

Bob's journal entry for June 5th read:

Rae Ann and the kids are with me in the North Woods of Maine! I feel more complete than I have in many months. Staying so active helps keep my mind away from the difficulties in Muhlenberg County. I know the problems will need to be addressed eventually. Having my family here gives me one less thing to worry about because I know they're safe. I need to enjoy the present moment and hopefully make a positive impact on the next generation.

10

NEW BEGINNINGS

The next morning was opening day at Camp Okimachobee. All the finishing touches were done, the camp was spotless and the supplies were in place. Claire and Henry were excited to see other kids their age. What they didn't expect was how different these kids would be.

At ten o'clock that morning they heard the deep engine of an approaching bus. It pulled into the small gravel parking lot and squealed to a halt. The first person off the bus was a plump boy with a round head and pale cheeks. He wore a thick metal chain around his neck, had on bulky headphones, flat bottomed tennis shoes that looked two sizes too big, with tongues sticking out from the shoelaces. He squinted in the sunlight as he came off the bus scowling.

"Hello there. My name is Bob Baker, I'm one of the camp leaders," Bob greeted the youngster enthusiastically. The greeting was met with silence as the hefty boy looked down at the ground rudely, and shuffled off to the side of the dusty parking area waiting for his friends to get off the bus.

The boy looked at Henry and Claire and asked "Where is the closest McDonald's?" The Baker children shrugged. The

Photograph by John Plescia

camper with "Harold" engraved on his metal chain belched loudly. The Baker children's eyes dilated and they looked away, smelling grease in the air.

As the rest of the students got off the bus, they did not look too happy to be there either. Bob looked at Mitch Cedar with a worried expression on his face. Mitch gave him a wink and a small head shake that said, *don't worry, this is expected.*

The last person off the bus was a 21-year-old man with brown shaggy hair, an athletic build, and DNR fatigues. His name tag said "Nick Ozburn" in black, bold-faced letters. He was grinning ear to ear, and stretched as he took a deep, full breath of the clean air. "Aaaah! Good to be out of the city," he said.

The bus driver honked the horn and pulled out of the drive as soon as the campers' bags were taken from the undercarriage.

"Hello and welcome to Camp Okimachobee!" said Mitch Cedar. "We are happy to have you here and hope you're ready for the lessons that you will learn. Many of you have had behavior issues in the past, but now you get a clean slate. Listen to your camp counselors, learn from Nature, and you will have a fun and rewarding summer."

Several of the campers rolled their eyes, but a few seemed interested, though they were trying not to look it.

Mitch began introductions. "This is Mr. Bob Baker and his wife Rae Ann, and their kids Claire and Henry. They're similar in ages to all of you, twelve and nine. They're up here from Kentucky for the summer. I'm Mitch Cedar and you already know Nick Ozburn from the bus ride. We are your camp leaders for the summer. This Old Man here will be helping at times as well."

The Old Man was leaning against a large maple tree, holding his walking stick, with a tentative look on his face.

"OK, now we will show you around the camp. Bring your luggage in here," continued Mitch.

Mitch led them into the main camping area and showed them the six bunk beds with name tags on each. He went through the roll call and gave each camper a name tag that matched the name on his or her bunk. There were two girls out of the twelve, and their bunk beds were at the end behind a divider. "Samantha" and "Penny" were labeled on those two bunks. Mitch continued through the cabin, showing them the bathrooms and the cook hall. Harold, the boy who had gotten off the bus first, raised his hand.

"Yes Harold?" asked Bob.

"Being in the cook hall makes me hungry," said Harold. "There's gotta be a Burger King, Wendy's, or McDonald's around here somewhere, right?"

Just then the campers heard a large toot from Harold and that same greasy smell drifted across the room.

"Oops," he said, with a big grin on his face.

"Well... no," said Rae Ann, purposefully ignoring the blatantly bad behavior. "We don't have any fast food here in the North Woods of Maine, but there are a lot of fish, berries, and a beautiful garden that will supply most of our meals."

"Oh no, I'm gonna starve to death," whined Harold under his breath to the boy next to him. The kid couldn't hear him through the loud music playing in his earbuds. His nametag read "Mike."

"The next thing we need to do," said Nick Ozburn, "is to get rid of these electronics. Give me your cell phones, iPads, and any other gaming devices. They are going to spend the summer in the closet. You kids need to be unplugged for a while."

"No way, man!" shouted the campers as one. "You can't do this to us!"

"Yes, we can," said Bob sternly. "This is for your own good."

The grumbling and complaining was palpable. Electronic devices had become an extension of these children and they grudgingly handed them over. Once all the electronics were confiscated from the campers' pockets and duffel bags, the group headed outside.

"Now over here is the shed with all our camping gear, canoes, kayaks, and fishing supplies. In the smaller shed over there we have the bows, arrows, and targets. Since all of you are ten to twelve years old you can participate in archery lessons. In fact, that is our first activity to get started with today," explained Mitch Cedar.

Nick gave a detailed lecture about how Native Americans used homemade bows, arrows, and arrowheads for hunting. Then they took out the equipment and explained how to draw back the strings. There was a lot of discussion about safety and responsibility. Next the campers lined up and took turns drawing back the bow strings. Then they got to fire arrows at cardboard boxes in front of a big round bale of straw. At first most of the arrows ended up short of the target in the grass. Sometimes they would slide under the grass and be hard to find. Some arrows hit the straw bale, and once in a while one would hit the cardboard.

Three of the twelve-year-old boys from Portland were standing in a group talking. The bows and arrows lay on the ground where they had dropped them. They had never practiced archery before and wanted to establish power over the counselors early on. They had pulled this trick many times on adults at home. If a teacher told them to work on a project in class or a coach told them to run a lap on the track, they would simply disobey. What could the adults really do?

Nick Ozburn approached them and cheerfully said, "Come on guys, let's participate. You don't have to be great at it, but you do have to give it a try."

The tallest of the three pre-teens said in a haughty tone, "We don't have to do anything we don't want to!"

The Old Man came running at them with his maple stick screaming, "Oh yes you do, you little punks!" He cocked back the stick, ready to whack some behinds when Mitch Cedar stepped in front of the scared boys at the last moment.

"Whoa, whoa, whoa, Old Man! We can be tough on these kids, but we can't seriously hurt them," said Mitch soothingly to the red-faced Old Man. He was clearly itching to paddle the misbehaving kids.

"In my day, if we EVER disrespected an elder, we'd get whooped!" pleaded the Old Man, with an angry eye on the boys.

"I know," said Mitch. "But things have changed a little. Don't worry, they will still learn to be respectful, appreciative, and try new things. We have all summer to teach this group."

The boys picked up the bows and half-heartedly shot a few arrows at the targets. They kept an anxious eye on the

Old Man who was pacing and glaring at them menacingly. He seemed a little crazy to them and they didn't want to instigate another attack, especially if Mitch Cedar wasn't close enough to protect them.

Mike had an instant knack for shooting the bow. By the end of their activity time, he was hitting the straw bale consistently and nailing the cardboard about four out of ten shots.

Mike was diagnosed with ADHD at age seven. He had been getting bad grades and was often disruptive in class. His parents divorced the year before his diagnosis. Since then, he only talked to his dad a few times each year. Birthday cards tapered off and now disappeared. His mom worked two part-time jobs. Mike took his Adderall twice a day. It helped him focus but didn't fix his restlessness or anxiety.

"This is pretty cool!" yelled Mike.

Nick glanced at Bob with a surprised, sheepish grin.

"Wow, he's pretty good," whispered Nick.

"No kidding," agreed Bob.

Later that evening Nick shaved, showered, and put on a clean shirt. He took the camp van into Allagash and parked on Dickey Road. After the long bus ride up from Portland and opening day at camp, Nick was ready for a break from the noise of twelve pre-teens. This was a good chance to check out the town.

Nick grew up in the outskirts of the Chicagoland suburbs

but always had an affinity for natural spaces. As a child, he would fish in a small drainage ditch in a wooded area by his house. He was currently on summer break between his junior and senior year of college at the University of Southern Maine Portland Campus. He was studying natural resources and environmental sciences. When one of his professors mentioned the Camp Okimachobee summer mentorship program, Nick jumped at the chance.

He liked the feel of this small town. Nick noticed the quaint restaurant across from the river. He stepped onto the boardwalk and saw the posted hours. They closed at 3pm and it was well after six. He peered in the window and saw a moose head, pheasant, and bobcat on the wall keeping vigil over the cozy dining area. *My kind of place*, he thought.

Just then he was startled by a female voice close behind him in the parking lot. "Can I help you?" she asked in a curious but stern tone.

"I... uhh... well... was looking for some food," he stammered. He couldn't tell if she was being helpful or thought he was breaking into the restaurant. He could tell, however, that she was strikingly pretty and likely in her early twenties. She was wearing cutoff jean shorts and a blue University of Maine at Presque Isle t-shirt with the Owl's logo and the words "North of Ordinary". Her wavy brown hair, shoulder length with hints of red in the evening sun, was glowing in youthful summer.

"You're not from here..." she replied, half question half statement.

"No, I'm going to school in Portland," said Nick.

"You're not from Portland either. Maybe Portland,

Oregon, but not Portland, Maine, not with that accent you're not," she said with a thin smile crossing her lips.

"Well, no... I um... I grew up near Chicago and I'm just going to college at University of Southern Maine in Portland." His mind and tongue seemed to be completely disconnected from each other. It was frustrating because he usually had decent command of the English language but couldn't tell if she was curious or accusing him of lying about where he was from? Maybe he was just very hungry? Or maybe it was the sunlight reflecting off the Allagash River behind her? Were her lips always that red? Or lipstick? Or sunburned?

"Oh, OK that makes sense," said the girl, fully smiling now. "Shicaaago, ayup that's true. Well, you're out of luck for food, we closed at three."

"Hey," said Nick grinning, as his brain returned to him. "You have an accent too!"

"Fair enough," said the girl. "What brings you from Portland up here?"

"I'm a camp counselor at Okimachobee for summer break," said Nick as his heartrate returned to normal.

"Hahaha, old Mitch Cedar putting you to work huh?" said the girl. "Are you doing OK with those rowdy kids?"

"They're not so bad."

"But camp just started today," said the girl with a pretty laugh.

"True," agreed Nick. "Maybe in a few days I can see you again to let you know how it's going?"

"That would be fine. We're open from 7am to 3pm."

"Who should I ask for?" asked Nick with raised eyebrows

and a half grin, thankful that the stammering spell from earlier had passed.

"Emma," she said, extending her hand. "I like the accent." She waved as she headed down the boardwalk ramp.

"Nice to meet you Emma, I'll see you again in the next few days." Nick took a deep breath and smiled as he headed down the street toward the van. "I like this town," he said under his breath to himself.

11

LIFE ON THE CREEK

The first night at the camp was a struggle for most of the campers. They were not used to being away from home and were a little worried about it. They were in cots and bunk beds, the darkness was solid due to the lack of streetlights, and the sounds were much different from what they heard in the city. The kids were used to traffic, sirens, and planes; not coyotes, owls, and the wind.

Harold whispered to Mike who was on the top bunk, "Hey man I don't know about this."

"I know," shuddered Mike. "This is spooky. We could disappear out here in the wilderness and no one would ever find us. There are no police even if we called."

Harold replied, "My parents were so upset with me for not listening and talking back, but I think they would feel bad if they knew they were sending me to a camp like this."

"My mom knew exactly what this place was about," said Mike. "My cousin came here three years ago. He is now a straight A student in high school and even volunteers at the nursing home. When he came back that summer, he didn't talk much about it, but said he learned a lot."

Photograph by John Plescia

The next morning at breakfast all the campers, including the Baker kids, sat at their assigned seats. Breakfast was venison sausage, whole wheat pancakes with flax seed and local maple syrup, chicken eggs from the coop, and fresh blueberries from the meadow. The campers from the city looked a little draggy and droopy eyed, but not one complained about the food.

Bob Baker announced to the group that today's activity is canoeing. "We will go to the shed and get the canoes ready. There will be one leader in each canoe with two or three campers. It is very important to wear your life jacket at all times and stay seated. There's a lot of snow melt which has the Kyte Creek moving pretty quickly. Listen to your leader and they will instruct you on what to do. Now clear and wash your plates at the big sink and stack them on the drying rack. We will meet outside by the shed in five minutes."

Five canoes were lined up and loaded with paddles, life vests, and one fishing pole per boat. Three canoes were green fiberglass and two were silver aluminum.

The campers, leaders, and the Baker children split up and filled the canoes. Samantha and Penny were in one green canoe with Mitch Cedar. They were not particularly excited about being out on a river. They were more used to going to the mall and the movies.

Penny whispered to Samantha, "This is sure going to be boring." Samantha nodded her head and rolled her eyes.

The canoes launched one by one into the clear, cold water of the Kyte. As soon as the current pushed Samantha's boat straight into the deep running water, she was no longer bored. Now she was just plain scared. The water was strong and the front of their canoe seemed to be tipsy and wobbly. Samantha was sitting in the front, Penny was in the middle, and Mitch Cedar was in the back using his wooden paddle as a rudder.

Mitch said, "Paddle hard and keep your weight low in the canoe, otherwise we'll tip for sure girls." He explained how to properly hold the paddles, with one hand at the top and the other in the middle, pulling the paddle down through the water.

They came around a curve and caught up with Rae Ann and three of the other city campers. Harold, Mike, and Henry were paddling hard with Nick Ozburn, who sat in the back seat of another canoe. Nick was explaining to them that the person in the back was mostly responsible for steering. The person in the front could steer a little by paddling hard on one side. The people in the middle were just for horsepower. There were yelps of excitement from the different canoes as the campers were electrified by the level two rapids and large waves.

Suddenly Harold stood up, looking back at the canoes following them and yelled, "Hey, this is pretty cool!"

Nick shouted, "Sit down Harold!"

It was too late. Just at that moment they hit a small rock and Harold was launched overboard. He dunked under and then popped up a little way downstream. He was trying to yell but the water was cold, and he was too scared to speak.

Mike yelled to his pudgy buddy, "I'm coming in after you!" He threw his paddle and leaped into the waves. The water was only three feet deep. Mike had a circular floatation device with a rope attached, which he flung to Harold. Then both the boys realized they could touch bottom and stood up. The bottom was rocky and slick but eventually they got their footing. Nick paddled over to the far bank which was nice and sandy. The other canoes all pulled onto shore there as well. The two wet boys made their way over to the group on shore.

"See why we say to keep seated Harold?" said Nick pointedly.

"Yes I do Mr. Ozburn," said Harold.

Next, they got out the fishing poles and waded downstream across from a deeper pool of water. Bob Baker taught them to cast at the high end of the pool and let the worms drift down through the deep water.

Henry was the first one to connect with a fish. "Ooooo I think I got one!" he yelled, as he started to reel it in.

"There you go!" shouted Mitch.

As Henry reeled the fish toward shore, they could see the bright colors rolling in the clear water. Then it jumped a foot into the air, and they could see the rainbow of colors and spots down its sides.

"That is a brook trout," yelled Bob, "and it is a keeper!"

"Good job honey," said Rae Ann.

Penny was the next to snag a fish and she gave a friendly high-five to Claire. It was amazing how once they started feeding, the fish were going wild. The air and water temperatures were starting to rise and that got the fish's metabolism up and they wanted to eat. Claire caught a nice brown trout that was in the legal range to keep. Some of the other kids caught small brookies and the leaders taught them how to gently release the fish so they can grow and be caught another day.

As quickly as the fish started to bite, it all stopped, as if a switch had been turned. Now they casted and reeled back in without even a nibble.

Bob Baker showed the children how to clean the trout. There were a lot of groans and several campers said "gross!" but they were interested and giddy with the adventure of it. Bob showed them the different organs and opened up the stomach to reveal worms, bugs, and crayfish that the healthy trout had recently eaten.

"Wow..." several of the children said, as they looked over his shoulder.

By the end of the day everyone was tired, sun soaked, and smelled of the outdoors. They loaded up the watercrafts and headed back to the camp to get cleaned up. Fresh air and exercise helped everyone sleep very soundly that night.

Nick Ozburn wished he could go to Allagash to find Emma, but he knew the restaurant was closed. He hoped there would be a chance soon to sneak away from camp duties and activities earlier in the day.

12

HEART HEALTH

Nick's chance to go back into Allagash came three days later. The camp activity for the day was *Intro to Outdoor Exercise*. Mitch Cedar walked through the bunkhouse at daybreak, waking up all the campers.

"Rise and shine punkin' heads," he said loudly but gently.

The campers moaned and rubbed sleep from their eyes. "What time is it?" "What's going on?" they murmured.

"Quick breakfast and time to work," said Mitch.

"Aaag," Mike groaned and buried his head in the pillow.

"No, no, no, Mr. Mike," said Mitch sternly, pulling the pillow from his hands. "Up, up!"

Five minutes later Mitch clanked the triangular chuck wagon food bell. The disgruntled campers trudged into the mess hall to find the Baker kids and four counselors eating a light breakfast of cold cereal and fruit.

"OK," said Mitch from the front of the room. "I know you are not thrilled about getting up early but there is a lot of truth to the saying *Early to bed, early to rise, makes a person healthy, wealthy, and wise.* Today we are working on the healthy part. The human body needs motion. We have to

Photograph by John Plescia

move. First, we'll get in a big circle outside and stretch as the sun comes up. I will stand in the center and lead the stretches, but it will all be quiet, no talking, just copy me. Be aware of the sun rising and the birds. There are yoga mats for each person. We will do different poses, pushups, sit-ups, leg lifts, and jumping jacks. Then you will all jog two miles on the forest trails. After that you'll walk the two-mile loop with a loaded camp pack, switching the pack to your partner at the one-mile marker. Finally, you will work together as a team to stack this pile of firewood in the shed. Once that is accomplished, you are free for the rest of the day."

Harold looked as if he might start crying. Mitch was flexible and had great balance. Some of the kids were awkward and this type of activity was very foreign to them. Samantha and Penny exchanged annoyed words and got a raised eyebrow "Shh" from Mitch. They looked dejected but did the exercises.

Harold was the straggler on the two-mile jog, red faced and huffing he plodded on. Claire and Henry led the pack and seemed to be racing each other, their competitive spirits showing. Claire's endurance was good from years of swimming, but Henry's thin lanky strides allowed him to keep up with his older sister for most of the run. She beat him to the finish line by twenty seconds. Mitch was waiting there with water and bananas.

Once all the activities were done, the campers were exhausted, but pleased that they were able to complete the tasks.

"Well done everybody!" cheered Mitch.

"That wasn't so bad," gasped Harold, but he looked like he might faint. Mike patted him on the shoulder.

"Hit the showers and you are free for the rest of the day," pronounced Mitch.

Nick got cleaned up and drove the van into Allagash, parking in the gravel lot next to Two Rivers Lunch. He entered the restaurant and his eyes adjusted from the bright sunshine outside. The sign said *Please seat yourself.* Most of the seats were full so he headed for an empty two-person table in the back corner. Emma was behind the counter taking a plate of food out from under the heat lamps when she saw him and waved.

"Who is that?" asked Mrs. Dumond with a smile.

"A guy named Nick I met the other day. He's working out at Camp Okimachobee this summer. From *Shicaaago* originally," said Emma smiling.

"Cute fella," said Mrs. Dumond, nudging Emma's arm playfully.

"Careful," said Emma laughing, "you'll make me spill the plate!" She delivered the food to a group of chatting, gray haired women, and made her way through the crowded tables to the corner.

"Hey Emma," said Nick.

"Hi there, what can I get you?" replied Emma, carrying a circular brown serving tray and white rag. She had a red bandana over her hair.

"I'll have a grilled cheese with hot sauce, fries, and an iced tea. Sure is busy in here."

"Yeah, pretty consistent lunch crowd. Not a lot of other options around here and our food is good," said Emma smiling. The older ladies were asking for a water refill so Emma said, "I better go, we'll talk more later."

"Cool," said Nick, watching her go.

Fifteen minutes later she came out with his food and sat across from him at the small square table.

"Thanks, looks great." He put ketchup next to the fries and said, "Help yourself," as he bit into the grilled cheese. "Mmm, that's excellent."

She ate a few fries. "So, what do you study?" she asked.

"Environmental sciences," he said between sips of iced tea. "I really enjoy the outdoors and science. Habitat restoration, that kind of thing. What do you study at U of M in Presque Isle?"

"How do you know I go there?" she asked, surprised.

"I noticed your shirt the other day," he said, smiling.

"Ahh, right," she said, blushing slightly. "I'm doing nursing and will be a senior in the fall."

"Me too," said Nick.

"What do you do for fun outside of school?" she asked.

"I like fishing, camping, hiking, reading, and frisbee golf," said Nick thinking.

"Plenty of those things around Aroostook County," said Emma. "What does your schedule look like for the rest of the day?"

"I'm totally open, no plans, no obligations, up for anything," Nick said quickly. He immediately regretted sounding overly interested, and then thought, *why hide the truth?*

"Oh good," she said, again faint blush rising in her cheeks.

"It's already 1:30 and I get off at three. If you don't mind a little drive, we can go over to Presque Isle and I'll show you campus. There is a great 18-hole disc golf course at Talon Trails Park. It takes about one and a half hours to get there, but I think you'd like the scenery."

"Sounds great," said Nick as he cleaned his plate. "I'll be across the street by the river. Just come get me whenever you're ready."

The three chatty women were waiting to pay their bill at the register. "I'd better go," said Emma, looking at the patrons. "I'll see you in a little while."

"Perfect, thanks," said Nick, wiping his mouth with a napkin and hoping there were no stray crumbs or ketchup on his face.

13

CHICKENS AND EGGS

Days turned to weeks in the easy flow of summertime. Camp Okimachobee held its yearly Food of the Earth Day. This was often cited as a highlight of the summer by camp graduates. The campers and counselors all started in the cafeteria as a group.

Mitch Cedar explained the agenda for the day, "The purpose of today is to show you where food actually comes from. Over the past few weeks, you probably have noticed that most of the food at this camp is grown, raised, or harvested close by. As the seasons change, so will the foods we eat. The wild blueberries and blackberries are straight from Nature. All we have to do is gather them. Deer, turkey, and fish have been the majority of the meat, along with the chickens and eggs. It takes a little work to keep the chicken coops clean and the chickens safe and fed, but the reward is great. Notice how little we have to buy from the store. That saves money and all the carbon pollution that comes from packaging and shipping foods long distances. It takes effort to keep the garden planted, weeded, and harvested."

"Sure does," groaned Harold with a frown.

Photograph by Trisha Plescia

"But Harold, look how you've grown to like spinach, carrots, onions, and lettuce," said Mitch. "You wouldn't touch that stuff when you got here. You were so used to eating pre-packaged, high-fructose junk foods. You've already lost ten pounds just being here one month. You must feel better?"

"Yeah, I do," Harold conceded with a shrug.

"Mr. Cedar?" Penny asked, "What makes syrup and honey better for you than high fructose and artificial sweeteners?"

"Great question," replied Mitch. "Humans evolved to handle and digest natural sweeteners in a much healthier way than more processed products. We don't know all the details, but it seems like our bodies release natural sugars into the blood stream more slowly. The normal gut flora, or the good bacteria that live in our intestines, seem to help digest natural products better than ones that are chemically made. Even with healthy sugars, moderation is a good policy. Now we will break into four groups and go to different stations, stay there for one hour, and then rotate. We'll break for lunch at noon. Mr. and Mrs. Baker will be at the chicken butchering station, I will lead a discussion on vine crops in the garden, Mr. Ozburn will lead tree nuts and forest mushrooms, and the Old Man will do beehives and maple syrup."

Samantha and Penny walked with Claire and Henry to the chicken coop, talking casually. Henry was tossing pinecones at his dad, who was playfully throwing them back at the kids.

Samantha and Penny were both twelve years old, about to turn thirteen later that summer. They were going into eighth grade. They'd been best friends since kindergarten, growing up in the same apartment building in Portland. The taller of the two girls was Samantha and the shorter one with brown hair was Penny.

Samantha's parents got divorced when she was in kindergarten and her dad vanished from her life. She always felt that it was her fault, even though her mom and the school counselors told her otherwise. She was an only child and her mom always seemed too busy to really listen. Samantha's grades slowly declined over the years, and her attitude worsened.

At least she had Penny. They were partners in crime, and a dreaded duo for the teachers. They talked in the back of classes and were rude to everyone. Their families were always tight on money, but both girls had the newest iPhones and expensive data packages. The girls recognized these unnecessary purchases as poor choices, but they liked to fit in. In a way, they resented their parents because the girls knew the devices were used as a way to keep them occupied. The girls just used them to disconnect from the reality at hand.

Penny was the youngest of five children. Her dad was a mechanic and her mom a waitress at a family diner outside Portland. They had met in high school, and got pregnant, and married shortly thereafter. With a baby on the way, any other plans they may have had were put on hold, and they both had to work. They put in maximum effort for minimal pay, and twenty years disappeared. They saw education as a means to an easier life for their children, so they emphasized it.

All their children excelled except for Penny. She had been born with a darkly pigmented, football-shaped birthmark on her left cheekbone. It was the size of a quarter. Doctors said it was benign and should never cause her problems. While it had never become cancerous, it sure did cause her problems. Classmates had been making fun of her since a young age. Relentless jokes and self-consciousness followed. She was sad and lonely with a mean, cold exterior. In second grade a girl called her "Penny the Dark Quarter Spot" and got a slap to the face and broken glasses for the comment. Penny got extra homework and a suspension. It had affected her personality and behavior to the point that she was at risk of not graduating to high school. Penny felt like a disappointment to her parents, but at least she had Samantha.

Bob and Rae Ann led the way to the chicken coop behind the bunkhouse. As they were about to get started, Samantha mumbled, "This is going to be stupid and pointless. We'll never do this at home."

Rae Ann spoke up, looking straight at the girl who was avoiding her eye contact. "Well, that is an interesting perspective, Miss Samantha. Look at people when they're talking to you," Rae Ann said sternly.

Samantha looked up. Her first thought was to fire back with a sharp remark, but the 35-year-old woman in front of her with a southern accent and strong tone exuded confidence and commanded respect.

"While you may not use this skill immediately or directly," explained Rae Ann, "butchering an animal that you raised teaches many lessons. Diligence, routine, and hard work. You are about to see the anatomy and biology of a living creature. You will learn how energy is transferred from the sun to plants to insects to chickens, and into you. A lot of the chicken anatomy is the same as humans, so you will learn about yourself as well. You will learn ways to cook healthy food. It is true that you may not be butchering chickens at your downtown Portland apartment this year or next, but how do you know you won't be living in a different place five years from now? I don't blame you for thinking this way. Summer camp is to help you kids think differently, so thank you Samantha for the comment. Any other questions?" Rae Ann asked, glancing over the small group.

Maybe it was the Kentucky accent, or the way Rae Ann locked eyes with her, or the way Penny nudged her in the arm, but Samantha said, "Thanks Mrs. Baker."

Bob smiled at his wife and began explaining how to raise chickens from eggs to maturity.

Bob's journal entry for July 3rd read:

I'm proud of Rae Ann for being such a strong role model for these girls. Claire and Henry have made some new friends this summer, kids they never would've met had we not come to this camp. I'm excited for fireworks tomorrow night, always a highlight of the summer. Hopefully, Tommy's doing OK out west. Any place is safer than eastern Kentucky right now.

14

MOVING TARGETS

Every couple of days, the campers practiced with traditional archery equipment. In the beginning this consisted of a lot of instruction from Nick Ozburn regarding history, stance, release, safety, and concentration. As the summer passed, the kids were more self-sufficient and spent most of the hour shooting independently. The campers' skill levels covered a full range, from those that seldom hit the target and had little interest up to Mike, who had continued to excel over the summer.

As they walked out to the targets one day in late July, swatting at mosquitoes and gnats, Mike said to Harold, "You know, six weeks ago I couldn't live without my phone and earbuds. Now I don't miss them at all, and I'd rather shoot the bow than play videogames anytime."

"It's crazy," said Harold. "I'd rather eat a venison steak than a BigMac. What happened?"

"It is all about connections," said Nick, walking up behind them. "Are you connected to people, Nature, and physical activity? Or Facebook, electronics, and the pressures of the modern world? It's up to us to decide what our focus is. Now let me see you shoot."

Photograph by Trisha Plescia

Mike nocked a cedar arrow to his Martin longbow, drew and released in one fluid motion. The arrow flew straight and drilled the three-inch bullseye at twenty-five yards. He repeated the process two more times, and the three arrows made a tight triangle in the bullseye. He did this despite bugs bouncing around his ears and sweat beading on his forehead.

"Wow!" exclaimed Nick. "Now what if we back up another ten yards?"

"Not a problem," Mike said calmly.

Harold handed him an arrow and he let it zip, straight and fast, to the bullseye.

"Man, that's awesome," said Nick. "You'll be ready for the tournament in two weeks for sure."

"What tournament?" Mike asked, surprised.

"Oh... I guess we didn't mention that," Ozburn said with a shrug and a smile. "There is an archery competition held August 15th each year outside of Allagash. There's a traditional division, compound division, and then moving shots. The prize is $500 cash for each division and a handmade Osage bow for whoever has the most points on moving targets."

"Holy smokes!" shouted Mike. "I've got to get practicing on moving targets."

"Right," Nick said. "We can go out in that big meadow by the creek, Harold and I will throw milk jugs and cardboard frisbees. We can attach a milk jug to fishing line and drag it across like a running rabbit."

They gathered the gear and the three of them headed off to practice. It was a free afternoon, so the rest of the campers and counselors went back to the bunkhouse to avoid the bugs. After an hour of moving target practice, the archers returned, showered, and then applied calamine and hydrocortisone cream to the worst of their bug bites. They also checked each other for ticks.

Mike's Adderall prescription had run out after the first month at camp. He was supposed to call his mom to get the refill sent, but he never did. He felt a little different without the medication but found he could still focus on things he enjoyed or needed to accomplish. This took effort but he felt healthy.

That night the Baker kids and the campers played guitars and harmonicas. They made s'mores around two campfire pits. The simple pleasures of childhood seemed to transcend time and place. Children from the city streets of Portland, Maine, or downtrodden eastern Kentucky could relish the innocence of melted Hershey's on sticky graham crackers in the North Woods of Maine.

Mitch Cedar, Nick Ozburn, and Bob and Rae Ann Baker sat talking on the front porch as fireflies flashed in the dark.

"Camp Okimachobee has been going for nineteen years now," said Mitch with a sigh.

"Such a great program," added Rae Ann. "We could sure use something like this in eastern Kentucky. Plenty of troubled kids. Just a lack of family structure, lots of drugs, and no good jobs."

"Yeah, it's easy for kids to go down the wrong path," said

Bob. "I think it's good you get them up here at this age because if you wait until high school, too much harm can already be done."

"We try to teach fundamentals and give them self-esteem building blocks during the summer camp, in hopes that they will apply it when they go back to their daily routines," said Mitch. "We've had a lot of success stories and some failures too. It is so great to get thank-you letters from families and campers. Sometimes we get them right away and other times it will be years later that a note shows up. When we get updates from this group, I'll share them with you guys."

"That would be great," said Rae Ann. "I'm really seeing a lot of growth in these kids just in eight weeks."

"You will love to see their final projects too," said Mitch.

"Yeah, tell us more about that," said Bob.

"We give each kid an idea of a project that they can do on their own or with a partner. We pick something that showcases their skills and that will help them solidify a valuable lesson they've learned here. They complete the task and sometimes present it to us or the community, depending on what it is."

"Oh cool," said Nick. "I think Mike could enter the archery contest in a couple weeks, since he has gotten so good with the bow and learned to focus."

"That's perfect," said Mitch. "I was thinking the exact same thing."

"I would like to send Penny and Samantha down Kyte Creek with camping gear and fishing poles. They can spend a night out on their own and we'll pick them up downstream," said Rae Ann. "That will teach them teamwork and self-confidence, which young ladies need."

"I got it!" exclaimed Bob. "Harold can prepare a healthy dinner for the whole camp. He's come a long way from eating Twinkies and Frosted Flakes."

"These are great ideas," said Mitch Cedar. "You folks have been a stellar team this summer. Thanks for all your hard work. Speaking of plans, what is your long-term plan Nick?"

"This will be my final year of undergrad," answered Nick. "And then I will likely do grad school for waterway restoration, and hopefully work for the DNR or Army Corps of Engineers. Find a cute lady to marry and do a good amount of trout and small-mouth fishing. Those are my goals."

"Sounds like a plan to me," Bob Baker said.

"I noticed you've been spending some time at Two Rivers Lunch, and it's got to be for more than the noon specials," said Rae Ann with a sly grin.

Nick chuckled, turning slightly pink.

"Ahh, to have so many options and youth on your side," said Mitch wistfully. "You just want to feel fulfilled with whatever it is you do. Don't be afraid to change course if needed. Your interests and expectations may change with time."

The group enjoyed a lull in the conversation, lost in their individual thoughts and watching the fireflies.

"Well, I'm beat..." said Mitch, standing up and stretching his lower back. He headed inside with a yawn.

"Me too," Bob and Rae Ann said almost in unison. "Good night y'all."

Nick was left sitting alone on a Leopold bench, hearing the campers running around and yelling in the freedom of the preteen years. He watched the night stars and felt the gentle summer breeze, thankful the bugs had died down, nostalgic for childhood, but looking forward to future stages of his life.

I wonder what will be tougher, catching a big smallmouth bass or finding a young lady to marry ? He smiled to himself, thinking of Emma and considering changing campuses to Presque Isle.

Photograph by Patrick Ruesch

15

ANTICIPATION AND SUCCESS

The days passed and the time left at camp grew short. It was August 14th and the day had arrived for Penny and Samantha to head into the wilds of Nature on their own. They had fishing gear, a two-person tent, a lantern, sleeping bags, and other provisions loaded. They ate a light breakfast and headed down to the banks of Kyte Creek. The other campers crowded around in excited expectation. It was a sending off, just like the old French Voyageurs and Native Americans did when families or warrior parties headed out on expeditions. The tribe wished them well and said goodbyes.

"To think we had never canoed or camped just three months ago, and now we are headed out on our own to cover thirty-four miles and spend a night out here!" exclaimed Penny.

"And I didn't even like to go outside before," agreed Samantha.

The morning was perfect- with sunshine, a faint breeze, and light dew. Rae Ann made her way through the crowd of campers carrying two wooden staffs. She resembled a female Moses, parting the sea of excited children.

"I have a gift for you two," Rae Ann said, holding out the sticks to the two girls. "I was going to give them to you tomorrow night but thought you may need them on your voyage."

"Wow," the girls said, as they admired the beautifully carved walking sticks. They were carved out of balsam fir, six-feet tall, and gently tapered at one end. At the thicker end was a drilled hole with a leather loop connected to a large, red carabiner with each girl's name and the date engraved.

"The old trappers used to navigate these waterways with poles like this. It's called snubbing down a river. When the water level is low like this, you can stand and use the pole to push off rocks and try to stick with the deeper channels. You still may need to get out and walk the canoes in some spots. You'll figure it out," said Rae Ann as the girls gave her a big hug. "I'm proud of you two. Now get going before we all start to cry."

The girls got in the canoe and the crowd pushed the boat into the water. Penny and Samantha raised their carved sticks above their heads and yelled, "Okimachobee! Okimachobee!"

As the canoe went around a bend out of sight, the waving campers chanted back in unison from the shore, "Okimachobee! Okimachobee!"

The girls paddled and poled their way down the late summer Kyte Creek to the confluence with the Allagash River. It was a full day of paddling in the heat. At the confluence they set up camp and grilled the trout they caught on a metal grate hung over the fire with a telescoping tripod setup.

"When we first came up here to the North Woods,

we were so afraid of the dark. We couldn't imagine being away from our phones for an hour, let alone months," said Samantha.

"Yeah, and look at us now," said Penny. "We are as wise as Sacajawea and as brave as Harriet Tubman!"

Meanwhile back at the camp house, Harold was busy preparing his meal for ten campers, the four Bakers, and the other counselors. He looked trim and more mature in his white apron and chef's hat. A little frazzled trying to cook a flavorful and healthy meal for seventeen people, but he was also in control and confident that he could pull it off. When six o'clock hit, he took a deep breath and rang the triangular dinner bell that beckoned everyone back to the cafeteria. The long wooden table at the center of the room was set with white cloth napkin place settings. The campers and counselors all filtered in like worker bees to a drop of nectar. They washed their hands at the slop sink and got to their usual seats. Mike set his bow and quiver in the corner and gave Harold a smile and thumbs up across the room.

"Hello and welcome to this edition of children's gourmet," said Harold in a deep steady voice. "For starters we have a spring green salad with pine nuts, fresh croutons, and raspberry vinaigrette dressing."

"Hey, Harold!" yelled Henry Baker. "It looks like some of your salad got in the water," as he pointed at the floating cucumber slice and mint sprig in each of the ice waters at the table.

"Yes," said Harold in an elegant French-sounding accent and a wave of his dish towel, "that is healthy, flavored water just for you my good sir. The two sides are potatoes and carrots, which many of you have helped weed and thin this summer. The main course is a venison meatloaf with seared pork bacon and barbeque sauce glaze."

"Yum, sounds good to me," said Bob hungrily.

"Remember the meatloaf granny used to make on Valentine's Day in the shape of a heart with red ketchup on it?" asked Claire Baker.

"Can't hardly beat Kentucky meatloaf," agreed Rae Ann. "Mama sure can cook."

The food came out in big platters and was eaten family style: a dish of carrots, potatoes, and meatloaf at each end of the wooden table and one in the center. There were big serving spoons for the vegetables and metal spatulas to serve squares of savory meatloaf. Everything smelled great and looked professional. The volume level of the rowdy campers seemed to dampen down when the food was served. Silverware clinking against plates filled the spaces between conversations at the table. The carrots were sliced like coins and had melted butter and a hint of brown sugar. The potatoes were red and white russets, the size of golf balls and smaller. They were the first ones harvested this season. They were boiled soft but not mushy, tossed with parsley, garlic salt, and a little milk and butter. The group enjoyed the meal immensely, and Bob noticed the chef observing his happy guests from the kitchen window. The proud counselor caught Harold's eye and gave him a wink. Harold pushed his lips together, nodded, and gave a confirming smile.

"Great food!" yelled a couple campers.

"And for dessert," started Harold...

"Wow you even made dessert? Thanks Harold!" complemented a younger camper.

"Yes, we have homemade ice cream, fresh from the udder this morning and churned this afternoon, with red and black raspberries." Harold went back to the freezer and returned with a metal rolling cart that held three trays of small bowls, brimming with the treats.

Henry and Claire each grabbed one tray and Harold took the third, passing out one bowl to each person. The campers sounded like they were seeing fireworks as they ate the ice cream and berries.

"Ooh!" "Yum!" "Excellent!" "Ahh..."

After the meal people washed and dried their dishes and slowly drifted back to their bunks. Bob Baker was thrilled with Harold's locally sourced meal and told him so. When all the kids had retreated to their bunks and the mess hall was clean, the counselors gathered on the front porch. Nick Ozburn got a campfire going in the pit just off the porch. They could hear faint guitar chords and singing coming from the campers' bunk house.

"I'll be right back," said Bob as he headed to his bunk.

"You know, I was worried about having Henry and Claire around all these 'bad kids' this summer, but it turns out they have had a blast and learned a ton," said Rae Ann.

"Yeah," said Bob as he returned up the porch steps, "like don't judge a book by its cover, second chances, hard work, enjoy people that are different from you." He pulled out a bottle from under his shirt. "Good ole Kentucky bourbon with a little added honey," as he took a pull from the bottle. He offered the bottle to the Old Man sitting to his right.

"Swaller Old Timer?"

"Don't mind if I do," he replied as he took a long pull "Ooh, that's a good burn," said the Old Man with a sigh. The bottle was passed along the half circle of camp chairs as the fire crackled. Even Rae Ann had some, and she seldom drank alcohol. It felt like a special occasion to everyone.

"I wonder how Sam and Penny are doing out there tonight?" asked Rae Ann, to no one in particular.

"I imagine they're just fine," said Mitch "They're good kids."

"Yeah," agreed Nick, "I just hope they do all right going back to their real-world existence in the city."

The group was quiet, contemplating their own thoughts, staring at the fire.

"Is Mike ready for the shoot tomorrow?" asked the Old Man.

"Yeah, I think he has a chance to do real well," said Nick. "He's come a long way from a mean little brat with no focus, to a thoughtful Buddha with a bow."

"The honey in this whiskey reminds me," said Bob, "how are those hives doing out at the cabin?"

"Well," said the Old Man, "that Mack and Joyce come around about once a week to add more boxes. Some are stacked up six feet high. I haven't seen that creepy One-Eyed Joe or Slim since we met them that first day. There are bees all over the place and twenty-five percent of that honey harvest at seven dollars per pound will certainly be nice. Honestly though, I'll be relieved to be shuck of that lot and I won't have 'em back out next year."

"Sounds good," agreed Bob.

"They can't be as bad as the Lewis boys by us in Muhlenberg County," Rae Ann said quickly. She didn't notice the uncomfortable look Bob gave her.

"Who are they?" asked the Old Man curiously.

"They are the ones that the Bakers have been-"

"OK that's enough," Bob interrupted, cutting Rae Ann off midsentence. "They don't all need to hear about that."

The fire burned low and crickets could be heard. Mitch announced he was going to bed. He stood up and stretched his lower back stiffly.

"Yep, me too," said Nick. "We've got a long day of archery tomorrow."

"Tomorrow evening we're going down with the truck to pick up the girls at the confluence of the St. John and Allagash Rivers," said Rae Ann. "Goodnight y'all," and the friends disbanded for the night.

As the Bakers walked toward their bunk, Bob put his arm around Rae Ann's shoulder. "Sorry Dear, I just don't want to have to explain all that, or even think about it this summer." Rae Ann nodded understandingly and wrapped her arm around his waist.

Photograph by Patrick Ruesch

16

CULMINATION DAY

August 15th came off gray and rainy. Mike woke up early with that nervous excitement similar to Christmas mornings. The archery tournament didn't start until nine o'clock. He went into the mess hall and made oatmeal and tea. A couple other tired campers came in and they all quietly ate breakfast. Harold came in and sat next to Mike.

"Morning Mike."

"Hi Harold. That was a heck of a meal last night," said Mike.

"Thanks man," replied Harold. "It was fun getting it together. How are you feeling about today?"

"I'm nervous," said Mike. "I mean, I'm confident that I can shoot but I really don't know how I compare to anyone else. I've never shot in a tournament, and these other kids probably do it all the time. Maybe compared to them I'm not any good."

"Well you're not in control of how anyone else does," said Harold. "All you can control is how you do, so try your best and let it fly."

"You're right," said Mike. "Thanks."

Nick Ozburn came in. "Hiya fellas," he said, taking a seat next to Mike and sipping at his coffee. "You guys about ready to head over to the shoot? It's a thirty-five-minute drive over toward Wheelock Mill, so let's load up and head over so you can warm up a bit."

"All right let's do it," said Mike. He got his bow and quiver and bug nets. Harold packed a lunch in a cooler, and the three of them got in the camp van.

They drove out of the gravel drive to the main blacktop road. They were mostly quiet as they cruised through pine forests and small farmsteads. Turnpike Troubadours "Goodbye Normal Street" played on the cd player. Nick checked the map on the archery flyer and eventually made a couple turns off the blacktop. There was a wooden sign hanging between two pines that read, *Wheelock Mill Field Archers: Open Tournament.* They pulled into the grass parking area. Mike gathered his gear and they walked up to the registration table.

"How many shooters?" asked the lady at the table.

"Just me," replied Mike.

"Traditional or compound?"

"Traditional."

"Under 18 or over?"

"Under."

"All right, here you go. Take this score card to the red course starting booth anytime in the next hour. They will pair you up and stamp your card for each round. The practice targets are over there, and plenty of concessions and vendors are back behind me. Have fun and good luck!"

"Thanks much," said Mike.

There were many archers and observers wandering around, stretching, and taking practice shots. Some were quiet and others swapped hunting stories and compared equipment and talked about the weather. The light rain had stopped, but the sky was still overcast and humid. Much of the crowd wore waterproof boots. The appearance of the archers was varied. Some wore army fatigues, some wore hunting camo, some had fancy compound bows with long stabilizers and fiberoptic sights. Others wore buckskins and moccasins; they carried handmade bows with leather quivers and cedar arrows with homemade knapped arrow points and turkey feather fletching. The archers ranged from young kids up to gray-haired seniors. Men and women from all over Maine, and even some from Quebec and New Brunswick. You could hear French and English coming from the crowd.

Mike shot about ten arrows into the practice targets at fifteen and twenty-five yards.

"Looks pretty good," said Harold from where he and Nick sat at a picnic table watching.

"Yeah, I feel good," said Mike.

After they pulled the arrows, they got a drink of water and walked to the table that had a red sign overhead.

"This is the qualifying round," explained the bearded attendant. "You shoot two arrows at each of the twenty targets. You get zero points for a miss, five for a hit anywhere, and ten for the bullseye. Traditional shooters need at least 200 points and compound shooters need 300 or more to qualify for the tournament. Mike will be shooting with Rich here."

The attendant introduced Mike to a man in a Yankees

ballcap carrying a black compound bow. With him was his young daughter, carrying a can of bug spray in one hand and a granola bar in the other. Rich was about mid-thirties with a medium build and a broad smile. Nick, Mike, and Harold all shook hands with Rich and the little girl.

The attendant added, "You exchange score cards now and keep score for each other. There is a line here on the scorecard for the signature of who kept score and the time the round finishes. You are not competing against each other obviously. Really just being the witness for each other's qualifying round. This will determine the seedings for the actual tournament. Good luck everyone. Any questions?"

"Nope," said both groups, and they headed down the trail to the first target. There were colored stakes for markers showing where to shoot from. There was a legend on the scorecards saying which colored stakes were for the different age groups and bow types. The targets were all 3D solid foam. Many deer, bear, wild hogs, and turkeys. The targets were set out along the trails and in the woods in natural poses.

The group got to a blue stake that marked the adult compound shooter post. Rich stood next to the stake and nocked an arrow. The group remained quiet and Rich fired the arrow – thwack! – into the deer's vitals. Bullseye! He pulled another arrow from his hip quiver and zipped it about three inches from his first shot, both clearly ten-point bullseyes.

"Nice shooting," everybody said.

"You got that deer for sure, Daddy," added the little girl.

"Thanks," said Rich with a smile.

Mike was thinking how incredibly different compound bows were from the traditional style of shooting. The compound was much more like shooting a gun. You draw, aim with the sights, then pull the release trigger. With the longbow, you look at your target, draw and release all at once with just a finger tab touching the string. The traditional equipment moves the projectiles at a much slower pace. All these thoughts were crowding his brain as he approached the red stake that marked his shooting location.

Mike positioned his feet about shoulder width apart, nocked a cedar arrow and looked at the doe target twenty yards ahead along the trail. He drew back and fired the arrow. Mike knew he had pulled his left hand slightly just as the arrow was leaving the bow.

"Dang it," he gasped, as the arrow nicked a buckthorn tree and glanced off into the brush.

"It's all right," said Nick.

"Shake it off," added Harold.

"Daddy, he hit that tree and the arrow went way over there," the little girl pointed.

"I know," said Rich quietly. "It's OK, shhh…"

Mike was flustered. His second shot was yanked low into the dirt between the deer's legs. The second target was a big strutting tom turkey. Rich the archer put two more shots straight in the little bullseye at thirty yards.

At fifteen yards, Mike's first arrow flew over the top of the target and splintered against some brushy trees. His second arrow nicked the turkey's tail feathers and ended up stuck in the dirt trail leading to the third target.

"That counts for five points, doesn't it?" shouted Harold.

Nick, Rich, and Mike all looked at the small print on the scorecard.

"No, I'm afraid not," said Rich, pointing to the writing. *Arrow tip must remain lodged in the target for points to be awarded.*

"Yep," said Nick, "that's the rule."

Mike looked dejected as another zero went on his scorecard, and they headed toward target number three.

Meanwhile Bob Baker, Rae Ann, and the Old Man were driving in the Bakers' rusty green Ford, headed to the take-out spot. Penny and Samantha had put-in at Kyte Creek on a Wednesday morning. It empties into the Allagash River, which then joins the St. John River. The girls were supposed to go through Poplar Island Rapids and take-out on the river right shore. The Bakers were going to drive on Old River Road and meet the campers near Allagash.

The three adults filled the front seat of the truck. The backseat and truck bed had been emptied to accommodate the two canoers and their gear. Bob was driving and Rae Ann sat between him and the Old Man. The clouds and rain from the morning had mostly cleared, and it was partly sunny and comfortable. The sun would shine warm when clouds were not obstructing it.

"We've been up here all summer," Rae Ann said, "and I don't know much about you Old Man."

It was obvious that she was genuinely wanting to know his story. Bob sat up a little straighter and glanced across to the passenger side.

"Not much to tell really, I'm just an ole trapper I guess."

Rae Ann noticed the Old Man's mood change, which was as apparent as the sun going behind the clouds.

"Oh, OK, OK, no worries," Rae Ann said, trying to avoid the awkward silence.

Thirty seconds passed as they twisted along the beautiful road.

"Well, I was born here," the Old Man started, staring out the windshield at the pines. "My dad was a logger and my mom grew up on a farm in Aroostook County. I am the oldest of three kids. I had two younger sisters. Susan died in Vietnam. There were eight female soldiers killed in that conflict, and my little sis was one of them. Her name is on the wall at the memorial. Broke our hearts. Sweet, tough girl, twenty years old, just kids we were. Sad what humans will do to each other. No different than the rest of the critters in the woods I suppose, just fighting, mating, and trying to survive and get our genetics passed along." He paused and Rae Ann patted his left shoulder.

The Old Man continued, "My other sister Rita lives in Bangor, see her every now and again. Well anyways, the timber industry dried up and Papa drove a semi then. I went to Northern Maine Community College. Studied biology. Met my wife there in Presque Isle. Karen, she was lovely. Nicest lady you'll ever meet."

He pulled out a faded picture from his wallet and passed it to Rae Ann. She saw a pretty young lady with red lipstick and wearing a summer dress. Brown hair pulled up in a tight bun.

"We met in a geology class and were married six months

later. Of course, all our folks thought that was way too quick. But we knew. We finished our associate's degrees and started working for the DNR. There were a lot of habitat restoration jobs, working on getting old clear cuts back to healthy ecosystems.

"We wanted to have a big family, but she just couldn't get pregnant. Very tough. Years passed. We lived in town, Allagash. Happy enough. She was thirty-two and I was thirty-three when she told me she was pregnant. I thought she was joking. We'd given up hope on that years ago. Sure enough, we had Ken that year. Heavy snowfalls pretty well shut down the county. Time marched on. Eighteen years later, it was March- she was diagnosed with breast cancer. Ken graduated from Allagash Consolidated school in May, and Karen died in August at age fifty. In fact, tomorrow will be twenty-three years since she died."

"Oh, Old Man, I'm so sorry," said Rae Ann, patting his shoulder again.

Bob Baker drove on quietly, taking it all in.

"I can't believe you have a son," said Rae Ann. "We've never heard you talk about him...?"

"Yeah, Ken and I have never been all that close. It seemed like he couldn't stand living here in the small town. He was never into the outdoors or sports, and that's what most people do here. Ken always liked theater and art. The high school didn't even have those things. As soon as Karen was buried and services were done with, Ken headed out to California. He always wanted the big city life. I guess New York was too close, he just wanted to get away. He went to LA and then San Francisco. That's when I moved out of town and built the cabin. Been there ever since. I only talk to Ken on Christmas."

The Old Man sighed wistfully.

"Not easy," Rae Ann said gently, and they drove on in silence.

Mike had two misses on target number three as well. He had to really start shooting or would not qualify for the tournament. He looked defeated, with slumped shoulders and slow gait. As the rest of the group walked down the trail toward target number four, Nick Ozburn pulled Mike aside.

"Snap out of it, dude," Nick said encouragingly. "You still have plenty of targets to qualify. You know you can do this! You've practiced all summer and I've seen you nail bullseyes consistently at this range. You've just gotta get your mind right. Block out everything and focus. You're a good kid Mike, and a darn good archer, now get at it." He slapped the youth on the back as they joined up with the rest of the group.

Rich had just fired his two arrows from the blue stake. Mike stepped in at the red stake and nocked an arrow. He took a deep breath, drew, and released. The arrow flew into the target.

"A gut shot!" yelled Harold.

The next arrow hit high on the front shoulder of the spike buck target.

"There you go man!" said Harold excitedly. "Another five points, so ten total on target number four."

Rich put the score on Mike's card. Mike glanced back at Nick as they approached target number five. Nick gave him a smile and thumbs up. Number five was a crouching bobcat. Rich hit it twice in the neck for ten points total. Mike breathed deep, drew, and released, placing the arrow perfectly behind the front shoulder in the five-inch diameter bullseye.

"Got it!" he said, pumping his fist.

His next arrow was two inches from the first, ten points each.

"Now I got it," he confirmed smiling.

Mike continued to shoot well. They got to target number 19 and he shot one bullseye and one five-point-hit for 15 points. He had 185 points going into the final target. Rich had reached his 300-point requirement back on target 17, so was relaxed. Everyone in the group knew that it came down to this last target to decide if Mike qualified for the next round of the tournament.

"You can do it," said Nick.

Harold just pumped his fist as Mike approached the red stake. Mike drew the Martin bow and fired on the ten-point buck at twenty yards. The shot looked good, maybe a touch farther back than ideal.

"Is that a bullseye?" Harold asked.

"I can't tell," said Mike.

Mike and Rich walked up to the target to look. The cedar arrow was stuck in the brown foam a half inch left of the bullseye circle, putting Mike at 190 points with one shot remaining. He smiled and shook his head as they walked back to the red stake. He drew the Martin and his left hand held perfectly still. It was a smooth release and he didn't move his hands until the arrow was solidly lodged two inches to the right of his first arrow.

"Yeah!" he yelled, jumping up in his calf-high boots. "I got it!" He smiled triumphantly back at Nick and Harold.

"Nice shot," said Rich as they walked to the big buck and pulled the four arrows.

They put in the final scores and signed each other's cards, along with the time and date. The group walked to the scorer's table and handed in the cards. Rich's daughter was playing on a pile of gravel by the parking lot.

"Goodbye fellas, good meeting you," said Rich as he walked toward the concessions.

"You too, good luck in the next round," said Mike.

"Ayup, keep at it, man," said Rich with a wave.

"Ahh..." sighed Mike with a deep breath as the three walked to the camp van to get their lunch.

The lunch consisted of peanut butter honey sandwiches on fresh sour dough, apples, granola bars, and water. After the quick meal, they went back to the scorer's table where a bracket was waiting. Only four traditional youth archers had qualified. Mike and a fifteen-year-old named Simon had tied with 200 points, so they were both going up against archers who had shot better in the qualifying round.

It was another twenty targets in a similar setup, except there were more varied shots. For example, number three was from an elevated tree stand, there was a seated shot, one was across a creek, one was a standing black bear between two oak trees with only its vitals exposed. There was a huge elk about sixty yards away down a hill. It was fun to watch and shoot this course. Mike was locked in and shot 280, easily beating his opponent at 230.

Simon lost to a thirteen-year-old French girl named Marie. So, in the championship round it was Mike against Marie. It was another twenty targets, but if you missed the first shot you forfeited the second shot and got a zero for that target. If you got a bullseye on your second arrow, you got to fire a third. If an archer reached three missed targets, they automatically lost the match. The pressure was high. Marie was one year older than Mike but a good half-foot taller. She was quiet and didn't smile at all when they were introduced and the rules explained. She wore a matching windbreaker to the two middle-aged men accompanying her. They walked ahead speaking softly with the referee who would score this round. The writing on their jackets was visible, *Canadian National Team*. Mike's eyes got as wide as saucers as he looked at Nick and Harold and swallowed hard.

Mike and Marie were even after thirteen targets, both shooting well with no misses. The Canadians looked nervous on target 14. Marie shot first and had two five-point hits. It was clear the men, one of whom had the same stern facial features she did, were angry with her. When Mike stepped up and drew on that target, one of the men sneezed just as Mike released his shot. The arrow dipped below the target into the dirt.

The referee looked at Mike and said, "Miss number one, zero on the card."

Nick Ozburn started to protest but Marie's trainer, Pierre, said, "pardonnez-moi," with a sly smile. "Les allergies," with a shrug.

Targets 15-18 were all even between the two archers, so Mike was down by ten points. By this time, both young archers were getting tired. Mike was happy he had practiced so much to keep up his endurance. The evening was wearing on. Geese were seen in small flocks, forming v's, heading south in preparatory flights, as if observing the silly human endeavors below.

On target 19 Marie shot both arrows low in the gut for ten points total. Mike drew and everyone watched the antelope target expectantly. Everyone except Pierre, who was behind Mike and tickled his right ear with a big bluestem stalk of prairie grass, shaped like a turkey foot.

"What the!" exclaimed Mike, as he twitched and launched the arrow into a gray boulder five feet from the target. The shaft splintered as the white nock flew into the woods.

"Second miss, zero points!" charged the ref. "One more miss and you are out, son."

"But he touched me!" protested Mike. "They're cheating!"

"I didn't see anything," said the ref, with a bit of sadness in his voice and his eyes.

Mike was down 20 points going into target 20 of the championship match. The target was a badger, small with a tiny bullseye three inches in diameter. Marie shot first and again got two fives, with both missing the bullseye by half an inch.

"Hahaha," Pierre cackled maliciously. "You need three bullseyes on this leetle targeet. Not going to happen."

Marie looked tired and seemed to have lost interest. Mike was zoned in on that three-inch circle, he was fluid, and smooth, nocking arrows and letting them fly, 1-2-3. They looked good, forming a tight triangle. The entire group of seven people ran up to the target. Two arrows were clearly in the circle, the third was on the line.

"No good!" shouted Pierre.

"Wait, wait!" said the ref. "It is breaking the line, it counts!" He showed everyone the rulebook.

"It's a tie!" shouted Harold.

Marie and Mike shook hands.

"What do we do about dis?" yelled Pierre.

It was not lost on anyone that the $500 prize was on the line.

"Well," said the ref, flipping through his rulebook. "*In the event of a tied score after 20 targets, then the moving target competition is the tie breaker.*"

Pierre turned to the other man in their group, who appeared to be Marie's father, saying, "But Marie doesn't shoot moving targets! That is not part of the standard Canadian routine!"

Finally, the green truck rolled to a stop beside the St. John River. In springtime the Poplar Island Rapids can be a raging torrent, but by mid-August it slows to mild riffles. The Bakers and the Old Man set up their camp chairs and watched the river, waiting for Samantha and Penny. The mosquitos and black flies were pretty bad and annoying. Rae Ann went back to the truck for head nets and bug spray. They even set up a tiki torch with citronella.

The Old Man gazed across the river to the far shore. He began speaking, as if to himself, while Bob and Rae Ann listened.

"There is no other way I could have learned these things... except by experience. The passing of time. My body is shot and my mind doesn't learn new things as quickly, but I walk more slowly, notice more, enjoy simple pleasures more fully. We learn from every experience. At 20, one cannot know what it feels like to be 70, but at 70, with thoughtful reflection, I can remember the feelings of being 20. If the Dickey-Lincoln dam project had gone through and The Allagash Wilderness Waterway wasn't designated, we'd be sitting under water right here. Much of our circumstances are an unravelling of chance."

Before they could comment, or even fully digest what the Old man had said, the canoe came around the river bend. Penny was in the front seat with her brown hair tucked under a mosquito net. Samantha was the first to notice the three observers on shore. She raised her paddle above her head and yelled, "Okimachobee! Okimachobee!"

The Bakers waved and the Old Man smiled. As the canoe approached shore, it was clear that they had been upcountry for a while. They looked tired but happy. Their hair was tangled, skin red with sun, wind, and bug bites, and plenty of dirt under their fingernails.

Penny carefully maneuvered the canoe into the small inlet where Bob was waiting to pull them onto solid ground. They got out and pulled the watercraft fully up on land. The girls were beaming with pride.

"Well... how was it?" asked Rae Ann.

Samantha and Penny both started at once to explain the adventure. Penny paused and let Samantha continue.

"We paddled hard for the first couple hours and realized we'd have to pace ourselves to make the full thirty-four miles. The canoe got stuck on a rock and when I got out to push us, I stepped in a deep spot and got soaked. It actually felt pretty good!" Samantha laughed.

Penny added, "That night we cooked our trout and sat around the fire for a while before going into the tent. We were almost asleep when coyotes started howling and yipping. They sounded so close, and like they were coming closer. It was spooky. Just then we heard something rustling in the bushes. It was pitch dark. Samantha was hiding in her sleeping bag…"

"I was not," interrupted Samantha. "I was just trying to stay warm!"

"Then why were you saying, 'I'm too young to get eaten by a coyote?'" asked Penny jokingly.

"Well maybe I was a little spooked," admitted Samantha with a smile.

"I had to go out with a flashlight to see what it was. I saw a pair of glowing eyes, a masked face, and a ringed tail. It was a raccoon getting the guts from our trout," said Penny matter-of-factly.

"Wow!" said Bob. "You're lucky it wasn't a black bear. That's why you always dispose of fish guts away from camp."

"Yeah, we figured that out after the scare," said Samantha.

"I certainly couldn't last out there for two full days," said the Old Man with a straight face to the girls.

"Because you're afraid of the dark and coyotes?" asked Penny.

"No, cause sitting in a canoe for that long and sleeping on the ground would kill my poor ole back," said the Old Man, playfully nudging Penny's shoulder.

The group continued talking while they loaded the canoe and gear into the truck.

"You two should be very proud of yourselves," said Rae Ann.

"We are," said the girls, nodding to each other. "We're very tired too, that was a long trip!"

"I can't wait to tell my mom all about it," said Penny.

"I'm going to write about this trip for a school assignment," said Samantha.

Everything was loaded and they piled into the truck. The sun was setting behind them as they drove back toward Allagash and Camp Okimachobee. Slaid Cleaves's "Horseshoe Lounge" played on the radio. Bob checked his rearview mirror and saw the two girls asleep, leaning on each other. Rae Ann touched his right hand and pointed to the passenger seat, where the Old Man was leaning against the door and snoring softly. A trickle of drool leaked into his gray beard. The Bakers smiled and held hands, enjoying the scenery and quiet drive.

The ref explained that there would be five moving targets and whoever had the most hits would be the winner. This was not just between Mike and Marie, however. The moving targets competition was open to all traditional archers whether they qualified or not, and there were no age categories. Five moving targets were presented to each contestant. Whoever had the most hits out of five won the beautiful handmade 45-pound Osage bow.

The ref explained that Mike and Marie may not win the moving target challenge if another archer did better than them, but it still acted as the tie breaker. For example, if Marie shot three out of five moving targets and Mike shot two out of five, then she would win the $500 dollar prize. If another archer hit four out of their five, then they would win the Osage bow.

Some of the archers had their own flu-flu arrows with big bulky feathers for the moving targets. This slowed the arrows down so they would not disappear into the surrounding woods. The Wheelock Field Archers group had some flu-flus for everyone to use if needed. Mike used his own. Marie's dad and Pierre were all in a huff about this format.

"This is not properly sanctioned, Marie never does this back-woods shooting nonsense," grumbled Pierre to Marie's dad.

No one else paid him any attention. Marie stayed with Mike and Harold, talking. About twenty archers all congregated at the edge of the field by the practice targets. One at a time, they approached the referee and gave their names. The archers stood ready with a nocked arrow and the ref whipped a plastic milk jug that had a little sand in it up into the air. The archer would draw and fire. Most arrows missed and arched harmlessly into the field, sticking into the soft ground. A few archers hit one or two milk jugs and the crowd cheered. It was tricky to get the timing down right.

Marie came to the line and missed all five shots – but was laughing and smiling the entire time. "This is really tough," she said, "but very fun!"

Mike came up and drilled four out of five milk jugs. Sometimes the arrow hit the target just as the milk jug was at its apex, other times it was already on its way down. The arrows punctured the clear plastic and the jug dropped to earth like a stuck bird. The crowd cheered excitedly.

Only two other archers hit three out of five, but no one did as well as Mike. After all the turns were done and the final arrows collected, the referee went to the microphone and announced the winners for each category. Mike was handed a $500 check and the amazing, handcrafted Osage longbow.

"That was a pleasure to watch, young man," said the ref, shaking Mike's hand.

"Thanks!" said Mike, "It was a lot of fun."

"Congratulations," Marie said. "Sorry about my dad and Pierre. They are so fixated on winning that they've lost the enjoyment of it."

"No worries, it was a good match. Take care Marie," Mike said, waving goodbye.

He was grinning ear to ear, carrying his prizes as they walked to the parking lot.

Nick gave Mike a big bear hug. "Pretty good for a kid with ADHD who everyone claimed couldn't focus, huh?"

"I couldn't have done it without all your help. It was a good day and a great summer," said Mike, getting into the van with moist eyes. He didn't tell Nick and Harold about his plan to give the check to his mom. "Let's get back to camp, I'm exhausted."

Photograph by Trisha Plescia

17

THINGS FALL APART

The campers had completed their year-end projects, said their goodbyes, and headed home to Portland, Maine the day after the archery tournament. Bob could feel the days getting shorter. Everything felt past its peak. It was Labor Day weekend, and the sense of early autumn was setting into the North Woods. More yellows on birch leaves, drying grass no longer thick and lush. Squirrels seemed less playful and more serious in their pursuit of nuts to hurriedly stash in shallow holes. Both dragonflies and houseflies seemed slower, evenings light dwindling more quickly than just three weeks before.

Mitch and Bob had been working steadily to clean and winterize the camp. Bob was happy that Mitch was a quiet worker like himself. They cleaned canoes and kayaks- and stacked them in the barn. They wiped down all the bunk beds and stored linens and kitchenware in plastic bins for the off months.

He knew he had to return to Kentucky. Rae Ann, Henry, and Claire had left several days ago to get ready for the new school year. Bob couldn't run from it anymore. Nearly a year in the North Woods had to be enough time to let things cool down. Otherwise, they would be winning, and he'd be running.

Meanwhile things were unraveling out at the Old Man's cabin. That morning the Old Man had come to town for breakfast and supplies. He ate at Two Rivers Lunch and talked to Emma. He purchased a cartful of flour, sugar, pasta, spices, and other essentials. He tossed a pack of gum and a newspaper on his groceries and paid the tab. He loaded the supplies into the back of his truck.

"Good boy," he said to Lou, ruffling his hair and ears as the dog sat contentedly on the passenger seat. The morning sun came in through the windshield and a pleasant breeze through the half-open windows.

They drove down the ten-mile, one-track lane back to the cabin. As they approached, they could see the big white semi parked next to the cabin. The Old Man parked close to the front porch and started unloading the supplies. Lou sat on the front seat where he had been during the entire morning trip. He had a look on his gray muzzle as if to say, "I guess there's nothing I can do to help so I'll just sit here and watch."

Through the back window of the cabin, looking out past the woodshed, the Old Man could see the four beekeepers loading pallets of beehives onto the truck. One man was using a forklift, one was on the back of the semi pushing pallets into place, one was lifting two to three boxes at a time and handing them to the man in the truck. The fourth man, who was clearly One-Eyed Joe, was leaning against the shed smoking a cigarette and barking orders and insults at the other three.

The Old Man just shook his head and scowled. He was not looking forward to talking to the beekeepers because it was obvious they were not expecting to pay him his promised share of the honey harvest. They were working quickly to get loaded and out of there before he could ask for the money. They were loading up all the hives, supers and hive bodies together. They were not even extracting the honey to see what they owed the Old Man. It made his blood boil to think of these scoundrels on his property.

"Darn stupid of me to even get mixed up with these guys in the first place," he mumbled to himself. "But I had no idea they were like this. I thought it would be good pollination and easy cash. Dang it!"

Lou sighed and looked up at the Old Man from his new resting spot beside the front door, as if to say, *"Again, nothing I can do to help you Old Timer."*

The Old Man knew he'd have to confront One-Eyed Joe to at least get some money out of him, but it looked like they still had a half-hour or so of loading to do before they would be ready to leave. He was dreading the confrontation, so thought he'd read the paper and rest first. It was a local Aroostook County paper that borrowed the national and international pages from the *Portland Press*. The front page was about the Labor Day Fall Festival of Straw Sculpting in Allagash. Local bake sale, auctions, obituaries, and crosswords. He was having a tough time focusing, knowing that he'd have to confront these four goons.

"Well might as well get at it, huh boy?" he said to Lou, as he haphazardly flipped through the pages. He came to the Portland section that featured an interesting occurrence, or fact, from each state in alphabetical order.

Alabama – hottest day on record... again
Alaska – huge halibut caught

.....

Maine – maple syrup record crop
Michigan – huge peach parade
Montana – Nature Conservancy purchases large easement for bison

With thoughts of his son Ken always in the back of his mind, his eyes glanced back up to California.

California – bee burglars back at it!

This caught his attention and he read further.

"We all know of disappearing colony syndrome where the individual bees die, but to have thousands of hives disappear, boxes and all? This is ridiculous!" a Napa Valley beekeeper was quoted.

"Throughout central California, thousands of hives have

gone missing over the past year. At first, we had no clues, but a security camera caught footage of four white bonneted bandits loading a yellow semi at a suburban San Francisco bee yard," said a local sheriff's deputy.

"It is not easy being a beekeeper lately," said the Napa keeper. "With mites and foul brood, and now people stealing hives... I'm ready to throw in the towel!"

The sheriff said that two weeks after that camera footage was collected, the vehicle was spotted at a toll booth on I-80 headed east.

"We searched Iowa, but that semi seemed to disappear into a sea of corn," said a state trooper.

"Ayup," said the Old Man as he glanced out the window at the last few white boxes. "That's got to be them."

He grabbed the lever action rifle from above the fireplace and loaded three shells into the magazine, jacking one into the chamber and putting a handful more in his jeans pocket. "Let's go, Lou," he said solemnly as he opened the door and headed around the house.

He walked quietly up to the side of the semi and scraped at some of the peeling white paint. Sure enough it was gold yellow underneath. He quietly eased toward the cab of the truck. The men were working on the other side. The Old Man stepped up onto the stairs and peered in the driver's side window. There were several different state license plates piled haphazardly in the console.

The Old Man and Lou could read each other's moods and expectations. Lou had spent his entire life with the Old Man, hunting and trapping, and working around the cabin. The Old Man trusted the dog would be as quiet as he was, or more so. He stepped around the grill of the semi with the rifle aimed at the first man he saw. It was Mac.

"Whoa, whoa, whoa!" Mac said, startled.

Joyce was right next to him, a big hulk of a man, dirty overalls sticking out from the bee suit. Close to 300 pounds of muscle, bone, and fat. He was picking up a 40-pound box like it was a child's toy. He instantly set it down and took a step backward.

"Stop right there," said the Old Man. "Not another step."

Slim was coming toward Mac and Joyce from the rear of the semi. "Hey, hey, hey," said Slim, putting up his gloved hands and giving his chronic wheeze. The front of his bee bonnet and white suit were covered with a nasty mix of gear grease, propolis, and tobacco juice.

"Easy Old Timer," said Mac with a newfound arrogance. "No need to lay heat on us. We're just packing up for the year."

"Where is Joe?" the Old Man growled.

"Taking a leak," Slim hissed.

"Where?" demanded the Old Man.

"In the woods," said Slim, his poisonous smile showing through the screened hood.

It is interesting what comes into a man's mind at different times. The Old Man thought how foolish humans' actions must seem to dogs. The morning had passed so pleasantly and routinely, and now Lou's owner is pointing a deadly stick at enemies? Then he thought of all the angry bees in the air. Their years' worth of toil for the queen and her brood, flower upon flower, mile upon mile, wings fluttering like his heart was now pounding in his chest. Being stolen by men in white suits. He hadn't even made the honey, but he was standing here with a rifle. The bees must be angry beyond belief.

Sweat was rolling down his back and sides. They had full bee suits on and probably had still been stung while harvesting these boxes. If bees were to attack him now, how could he keep the rifle on these guys? And where was One-Eyed Joe? All of this passed through his mind. He couldn't tell if this was over seconds, minutes, or hours. Was it really this hot out? Or was it the glaring sun? Or the circumstances? Or his heart? It felt like freezing to death in Lake Marie or running ten miles back to town, which he wanted to do right now, but he couldn't do that, not now or ever again. He wanted to cry, and felt like he was, but it was just sweat rolling into his eyes. It stung, but he didn't dare take his hand away from the trigger. This was a young man's game. These heroics. Why did he come out here with a gun? He could've driven to town and gotten Sheriff Ted Thompson.

"Put the gun down," said Slim soothingly as he stepped forward.

The Old Man wasn't sure if it was the sound or Slim's movement that snapped him back to the present.

"Take one more step and this .243 will cut you in half, cowboy," said the Old Man, with more confidence than he was feeling.

Lou was growling with bared teeth at the three thieves. The Old Man was thankful for that. Slim's darting glance over the Old Man's right shoulder was his only warning. The Old Man followed that glance as One-Eyed Joe barreled into him. Joe's right shoulder crashed into the Old Man's right flank, and Joe's left hand whipped a pistol across the Old Man's right temple. The two blows were shocking. Ribs crunched and scalp lacerated, he tumbled to the ground beside the semi, out cold. Lou bit at One-Eyed Joe, tearing his pants and leaping at his throat. Joe transferred the .38 pistol to his right hand and put up his left forearm to guard his face. The dog's teeth sank into the thin bee suit and flesh. Joe howled in pain and pushed the gun barrel against Lou's skull just behind the ear and pulled the trigger. The gun jerked and the dog went limp and fell beside his master.

Back at Camp Okimachobee, Bob and Mitch Cedar had finished the cleanup for the year. Bob had packed his gear and the two men sat on the porch drinking a summer shandy and eating peanuts from the shell.

"Well, we did it," said Mitch. "Another successful year. I'm so happy you and Rae Ann and the kids were here."

"Thanks," said Bob. "It was an amazing experience. We all learned so much and it was a heck of a lot of fun."

"What's your plan now?" asked Mitch.

"If you can drive me to Allagash, I'd like to walk from there out to the cabin, just like I did back in the winter. You know, kind of come full circle. Get to see the land again as it heads into autumn. I'll gather my stuff from the cabin, help the Old Man with any chores, and head back to Kentucky in the next couple days."

"Sounds good," said Mitch.

They finished their beers and drove in Mitch's truck to town.

"Oh man! Did you kill him? Hehehe..." asked Slim, full of nervous excitement.

"He bit me, yeah I killed him," said One-Eyed Joe coolly.

"No, he means the Old Man," added Mac.

"I don't know if he's dead or not, check his pulse," Joe demanded.

"Still got a pulse. Look how it's pulsing blood out of his head!" laughed Mac.

"Cut it out," said Joyce. "Yeah, he's got a pulse," he added, feeling his wrist.

"I think we need to get him to a hospital," said Slim nervously.

"You're not paid to think gosh darn it, you're paid to work!" yelled Joe into Slim's veiled face. "Now get these boxes loaded and let's get out of here!"

The semi-trailer was nearly full of bee boxes and plenty of bees flying around. There was about four feet of empty space between the semi door and the last loaded boxes.

"Put the man in that space," ordered Joe.

"I don't feel good about this," said Joyce. "We are already

wanted for robbery. I don't want murder on my rap sheet. He could bleed to death or get stung up in there."

"Listen," said Joe coldly, "we ain't leaving him here. If he wakes up and blabs to the cops, we are hosed. We drive a couple hours, drop him on the side of a busy road somewhere, and some other sap will take him to a hospital. He'll never remember what happened or who we are. He ain't our problem."

"Right, hehehe," coughed Slim.

"Shut up," said Mac, slugging Slim. "Let's roll."

Bob Baker walked down the dirt track toward the cabin. He wondered how Rae Ann and the kids were. He wondered what the Lewis boys were up to. Had they drifted or ended up behind bars? Was Tommy still laying low out west? He again focused on his breathing and brought his mind back to the present. "Let Nature calm you," he said to himself. "Some things are out of our control."

He had been walking at a decent pace for about an hour when he heard the distant drone of an engine. It was coming toward him from the direction of the cabin. *"Probably the Old Man comin' to town,"*- thought Bob. But as a minute passed, he could tell the approaching vehicle was diesel powered and larger than a pickup. He caught a glare off the semi's windshield in the late afternoon sun. *"Geez, must be those dirtbag beekeepers."* The white semi barely slowed down, and Bob had to stumble into the brush to avoid being hit. He could see four faces packed in tight across the bench seat through the windshield. He caught a glimpse of Mac near the passenger side door, sneering down at him and flipping the bird.

"Jerks!" yelled Bob as he got back to his feet on the edge of the road.

He continued on toward the cabin. The sun was in the western sky when Bob neared the turnaround driveway. The tall pines to the west of the cabin cast shadows on the open door, which was squeaking softly in the faint breeze. Bob knew at that instant something was terribly wrong. The Old Man would never leave the door open like this.

Bob ran into the house shouting, "Old Man! Lou! Where are you guys?" The newspaper lay open on the wooden table. Bob ran outside and around the back. He noticed at once that the hives were gone. A few empty pallets lay around.

And there was Lou's body. "No!" yelled Bob. He crouched down and felt the body. Rigor mortis was setting in. A pool of coagulated, purplish blood was in the grass under the dog's head. Bob looked around quickly and didn't see the Old Man or anyone else.

He ran back in the house. Other than the newspaper everything looked in order, as if the Old Man had just stepped outside. Then he noticed the rifle was gone from its hooks on the wall. The box of shells was empty too. He felt frantic but made himself sit at the wooden table and drink a glass of water. His mouth was dry from the long walk and the shock of the scene.

It didn't take Sherlock Holmes to deduce that One-Eyed Joe and his goons had killed Lou and likely taken the Old

Man, if he wasn't already dead or injured in the woods nearby. Bob finished his water and walked a few circles through the clearing, fur shed, and surrounding woods, but couldn't find any signs. He then went out to the Old Man's truck and found the keys on the cluttered dash. The semi had an hour's head start on him and there were only about two hours of daylight left.

"Where are they headed?" Bob asked himself. "They killed Lou and if they hurt that Old Man so help me there will be hell to pay."

He considered calling the police, but it was a fleeting thought. Ted Thompson probably wouldn't believe him anyway. Bob wanted revenge and justice – quick justice, forceful justice – and taking matters into his own hands was the only way Bob Baker knew how to operate.

18

REST IN PIECES

The semi cruised through Allagash on Route 161, headed northeast.

"What's the plan boss?" asked Slim.

"We're putting distance down," said One-Eyed Joe. "We'll drive through the night, then pull off somewhere in the Green Mountain National Forest and lay low for a couple days, repaint the semi, and then slowly keep heading west to Pennsylvania where we can sell the hives. Once we cash in, we'll disburse and meet back up in California to steal another load."

"What about the Old Man?" asked Joyce.

"Oh yeah I forgot about him…" answered Joe. "We'll dump him out somewhere this evening."

"Maybe we should give him some water?" asked Joyce.

"You crybaby," said Mac. "We ain't stopping. That dang Bob Baker guy probably got to the cabin by now. He's going to get back to town and call the cops. It will take them a few hours to investigate but they'll be patrolling for us before too long."

"Right," said Joe. "By then we'll be nestled in the woods

Photograph by Trisha Plescia

in Vermont and this whole thing will blow over. We'll drop him off when we have to stop for gas anyways. I'm not making an extra stop. If little Joyce doesn't like it, we can pitch him and the Old Man out the door right now."

Joe's one eye glared at Joyce, and Joyce shivered despite the hot stuffy air in the tight cab.

"All right all right," croaked Joyce.

The fear of Joe's wrath was part of his concern, but the more immediate fact was that they were barreling down a narrow two-lane blacktop at 70 miles per hour with a heavy load, hemmed in with trees and mailboxes, and Joe's one lazy eye had been off the road for a long five seconds as if he didn't care one bit if they crashed and died in a fiery ball of metal.

"Ha! That's better little Joyce," cackled Joe as he pounded the steering wheel, thoroughly enjoying making the big man squirm.

Bob covered the ten miles from the cabin to Allagash in about eight minutes, as fast as he could go without careening off the old logging road. His mind was racing equally as fast, trying to picture what the criminals would do. It was just like how the Old Man had taught him to track and predict animals in the woods and trapline. This was the most dangerous species of all- humans. The same survival instincts of every other animal but with a huge frontal cortex, memories, emotions, hurts, habits, hang-ups, jealousy, traumas, bitterness, anger, and abuses from how we treat each other. Bob was tracking One-Eyed Joe because Joe was the brains and leader of the group. The decisions flowed from him like poison. Bob would feel better about going in a cave after a cougar or rattler than following this buzzard, but it was the dealt hand of the moment.

Bob stopped at the Main Street stop sign and got out the road atlas. The route was no mystery. There was nothing but wilderness in every direction except east. The thieves would be running like a scared white-tailed buck. *Escape! Escape! Escape!* The only road out of town was 161. The criminals couldn't go north or west because they would be at the mercy of Canadian border patrol. They would take Route 161 to Route 11 and go south to I-95. It was really the only way to cover ground quickly. Bob hit the gas and cruised through town. He didn't want to go so fast that he'd get pulled over, but the semi had a one-hour head start so he had to gain ground. The big 18-wheel rig could go 60-70 mph, so he had to go 70-80 mph, no way around that. It would take luck to catch them with out getting into trouble with the authorities himself.

Sheriff Ted Thompson was walking out of the drugstore when the Old Man's truck sped through town. He clearly saw Bob Baker in the driver's seat, lean faced, with no one in the passenger seat. The sheriff had known Bob nearly a year, but his first thought was the prison history. *Where was the Old Man? Why was Bob speeding?* It was a three-block walk to his office and he would call the police station in Masardis.

When he got to his phone he paused. Bob Baker had been hard-working and seemed honest and friendly. Thompson had dealt with many criminals over the years and knew they could put on a good show. When a law was broken it was the sheriff's job to make an arrest, not to consider the circumstances or possibilities.

He picked up the phone.

Bob pushed the pedal down and flew through St. Francis, Saint-Francois-de-Madawaska, and rolled into Claire, Maine turning south on Route 11. Sometimes luck is bad, and Bob Baker had his share of that. But sometimes it is good, and without him knowing it, the weather seemed to be in his favor. Nature knew nothing of these human trials and desires going on in northern Maine, or California, or Quito, or Burkina Faso, or Jaipur, or any other place. All Nature knew was that a low-pressure system moved across the Great Lakes two days ago, pulling up moisture. Winds picked up pushing east through central Maine and the temperature was plummeting as the front hit the town of Medway and it poured down in sheets.

The semi had just pulled onto I-95 at Sherman when it started raining.

"Dang it!" cursed One-Eyed Joe.

As red taillights started glowing on and off, he had to slow down. The four thieves felt slightly safer with visibility so low. It seemed like no one would be in pursuit and couldn't see them even if they were. Traffic piled up in the torrential downpour. Five miles ahead, a Toyota Tacoma rear-ended a Honda Odyssey and that reduced the pace even more with one lane totally blocked. The windshield wipers were going *slap slap slap* at full tilt as the semi crawled in thickening traffic.

"Masardis PD," answered the receptionist.
"Hey this is Chief Thompson up in Allagash. Is Lieutenant McPharson in please?"
"Yeah, I'll get him, just a minute."
Several minutes passed.
"Ayup, yello, this is Patrick, what's up?" answered the thick, slow voice, donut crumbs falling past his chocolate-stained chin.
"Yeah, hey Pat, this is Ted. So, we've had this ex-con named Bob Baker around here this past year. Seems like a decent guy but I think he just stole a truck. He sped through town in a red Chevy pickup that doesn't belong to him."
"Who's it belong to?" asked the Lieutenant.
"It belongs to an Old Man, trapper outside of town, good ole boy getting up in age. Anyways, the Old Man wasn't in the truck," explained Ted.
"Well maybe he was borrowing it," said Lieutenant McPharson.
"Well...yeah maybe," said Ted Thompson. "But he looked

awfully serious and he was clearly speeding. I don't know, but I don't like it. Just watch out for him, I get the feeling he's headed your way."

Sheriff Thompson heard coughing and sputtering on the other end of the line. Lieutenant McPharson spit his coffee as he brought his feet off the dash, spilling half of it on his big, crumb-covered belly. His eyes got as big as saucers.

"Holy Hannah, there he goes!"

The red Chevy pickup flew down the country road at 85 mph right past the hidden cop car.

"I'm on him!" yelled Lieutenant McPharson as he turned on the wailers and lights and spun his tires on the loose gravel.

In his flush of unexpected excitement, spilled coffee, and half-eaten donut, the fluster-prone cop didn't see the loaded logging truck barreling down from the north. The trucker nearly wet his pants to see a cop car pull out of the woods thirty yards ahead of him. He slammed the brakes and jack-knifed. Physics cares about human plans as much as Mother Nature does. The inertia spilled three-foot diameter white pine logs across the road in front and behind the esteemed lawman's car.

"Dang it all!" yelled McPharson, as his radiator burst and steamed all over in the middle of the road.

Bob Baker could see the clouds crushing in to the south. He smiled slightly as he started to think he had a chance to catch the thieves. He worried about the Old Man- he'd become a father figure to him over the seasons. As he approached the highway onramp at Sherman, he could see the red taillights through pouring rain.

"Here's my chance," Bob said to himself as he pulled onto the right shoulder and sped past the crawling cars.

He didn't even notice the angry looks from other drivers because he was straining his eyes looking for the white semi. Bob slowed down by a couple stopped semis, but when he got alongside them and could see the license plate or inside the cab, he knew it wasn't the beekeepers. By now it was dark and with the rain, visibility was very difficult. Some highway lights helped. When there were no similar looking semis to check, he could speed down the paved shoulder more quickly. The fuel light on the dash switched on.

"Dang it, not now!" Bob cursed.

Just then there was a rest stop exit. *"I have to keep going,"*- Bob thought. As he drove along the shoulder and passed the exit, he glanced off toward the rest stop building and parking lot. It was well lit and at the far end of the rest stop was the semi.

"That's it!" yelled Bob. "You buzzards are going to get it."

He turned off the highway, going the wrong way on the re-entrance ramp. Bob wasn't thinking, wasn't planning, he was just going. He didn't feel tired or scared, just angry and dangerous. Adrenaline coursed through his vessels and the response in his nerves, muscles, and eyes was primitive and real. He hit the brakes and slid on the wet pavement to a halt beside the semi. Bob stepped onto the black grate steps of the semi, which the Old Man had stepped on hours before, to peer into the cab.

Bob flung open the driver's door and tightly grasped the shirt collar of One-Eyed Joe with his left hand. To say Joe was shocked was an understatement. He was half asleep and wasn't expecting a raging maniac to come out of the rain. Bob Baker pulled him down the steps into the wet night. Under the streetlight, Bob was jerking him violently, Joe's head hitting against the corner of the trailer and pulling him forward into his flashing right fist repeatedly. Joe's nose crunched, lips split, face pummeled. Once the initial shock in Joe's brain subsided his natural drive was for survival. His left hand tried to protect his face and loosen Bob's iron grip around the collar. Bob's knuckles were pushed so tightly into Joe's Adam's apple, he could barely breathe. Joe's right hand slipped behind him and felt for the pistol in his waistband. He grabbed the handle, it was still loaded after shooting Lou that afternoon, and pulled it forward with the barrel pointed at Bob's abdomen.

The blasting force of Bob's fist against Joe's face was staggering. There was a blowout fracture of his eye socket, it was like a 90-mph fastball hitting his remaining good eye. The globe burst, circuits went out, the wet metal handle of the gun slipped from his fingers and fell in the oily puddles of the parking lot. No-Eyed Joe crumpled to lie still on top of the .38 pistol.

Just then the weasel-like Slim came around the back of the semi, swinging a five-foot 2x4 at Bob's head. Bob jumped toward the attacker and the board hit him hard in the right ribs under his right arm. He could feel his ribs break but kept his arm clamped down on the piece of wood to prevent another swing. Bob jerked the wood out of Slim's hands just as big Joyce growled, coming around the front of the semi at Bob. Bob kicked downward at Joyce's kneecap and with the weight of the bigger man coming forward, it increased the damage. Bob could feel the ligaments give way as the knee hyperextended and bent inward against its usual range of motion. Joyce howled in pain and fell to the wet pavement, clutching the ruined joint.

As Bob's back was toward Slim, the thin criminal pulled his hunting knife and ran in for the kill. Bob was just turning to face his attacker when the blade cut down on his right shoulder. It cut through his shirt and seared like red hot iron across his trapezius and right deltoid muscles. His scapula and the fact that it was a glancing blow saved him, preventing the blade from penetrating into vital organs.

"Aarrggraa!" yelled Bob as his days of high school wrestling fifteen years before came instantly back to him.

Slim's momentum was coming forward and both men were slightly unstable on the wet ground. Their clothes were soaked with rain and Bob's entire right side was a bloody mess by now. The pain was almost nothing in his brain as the primal drive to fight was unleashed, for the Old Man, for Lou, for his brother, for misfortune, and for misdeeds. The two men grappled like animals. Bob took him down with a single leg and fought to get hand control, avoiding the blade.

Slim was surprisingly strong for such a thin man. He was wiry and knew that having a knife gave him the upper hand. Slim also knew that it was only a matter of minutes before Mac came back from the bathroom and could easily take out Bob Baker. There were no other people around except for the customers at the rest stop building, and this fighting was happening at the far end of the lot, hidden behind the semi and steady rain. Slim was on his back and Bob's left hand held Slim's right wrist with the knife pinned against the ground. Slim's left hand was free, reaching for Bob's neck and eyes. At one point, Slim's fingers were in Bob's mouth and he bit down hard. They grunted and coughed. It was a fight to the death.

Just then Slim's long legs flung up and one heel caught around Bob's face and pulled him backward roughly. Now Bob was on his back gasping. Slim lurched at him with the knife slashing at his face. Bob's right hand luckily landed on the discarded 2x4 and pulled it between himself and the thug. The blade buried into the wet wood inches from Bob's face. Having the sharp weapon out of the equation, Slim's confidence evaporated. Bob sat upward so suddenly his head nailed Slim's chin, jamming his mandible closed, giving an instant concussion. Bob grabbed Slim's throat and rolled over on top of him. Bob pushed his right forearm onto Slim's thin neck, cutting off his air. Slim gasped wide-eyed and was getting cyanotic at the lips.

Bob was so focused on the fight at hand he didn't hear Mac run to the semi's passenger side door and grab the Old Man's rifle. He also didn't hear the Aroostook County police car roaring toward them through the rest stop parking lot.

Mac swung the barrel of the gun down viciously on the side of Bob's head. It was an explosion of fireworks in his cranium. He felt himself falling off Slim's limp body but it felt like time slowed as he tipped over toward the wet ground. It was foggy outside and inside his brain as he lay with his right cheek in a puddle, eyes open. Everything echoed, sights and sounds in slow motion. He fought to maintain consciousness.

It was a losing battle, but before he faded he heard Sheriff Ted Thompson yell, "Drop it!"

Bob saw Mac raise the .243 and fire twice, working the lever action between shots. He heard two pistol shots from Ted and saw Mac drop the gun and stumble backward into the tailgate of the semi and fall to the ground. Then it was darkness.

19

RECOVERY

When Bob Baker opened his eyes, he was in Millinocket Hospital. It took him a full five minutes to remember what had happened and where he was. A wave of relief washed over him when he glanced to his right and saw the Old Man, pale and breathing quietly in the hospital bed beside him. Bob had an IV pole on the left side and large bandages on his right shoulder.

"Hey there, sleeping beauty," said Ted Thompson with a smile from a chair in the corner of the room.

Bob smiled and dozed back to sleep, feeling much more comfortable that he and the Old Man were finally safe.

When he opened his eyes again, it was to sunshine pouring in through the hospital blinds. Bob had no idea how much time had passed since the stormy night of fighting or since he had seen Ted Thompson in the corner chair. Based on the intensity of the sun, it was around midday. Just then a hospital worker came in with two trays of food.

"Lunchtime fellas," she said pleasantly, leaving one tray next to each patient.

Her voice woke up the Old Man and he rolled over to face

Photograph by Trisha Plescia

Bob. His face looked even older, tired, and lined. When he saw Bob, he smiled, and the twinkle returned to his faded blue eyes.

"Heya, Bob," said the Old Man.

"Hey Old Man," answered Bob with a smile. "Let's eat, I'm starved."

They each took the plastic lids off the food. Chicken strips, mashed potatoes, canned green beans, and iced tea. After they finished eating, they both sat up a little in bed and kept sipping the iced teas.

"So, what happened out at the cabin?" asked Bob quietly.

"Well… I got out there and they were loading the hives, clearly not intending to pay me. Then I saw in the newspaper that they were wanted criminals. I went out to confront them and One-Eyed Joe snuck up and pistol-whipped me. That's all I remember."

The men were quiet for a few minutes digesting the food and the revelations.

"Lou?" asked the Old Man.

"No," said Bob with a shake of his head. "I found him behind the cabin, shot."

The Old Man looked out the window and began sobbing.

They slept away the afternoon and woke up for their evening meal. Shortly after the trays were delivered, a young doctor in a white coat came in with a stethoscope around her collar and a brown ponytail flipped out the back.

"Good evening gentlemen, you look more alive than you have been all week," she said with a friendly smile. "I'm Dr. Butler, the hospitalist that has been taking care of you here. Mr. Old Man, you gave us quite a scare. Now due to privacy rules, HIPPA, I must ask are you OK with me explaining your medical histories in front of each other, or would you prefer we talk individually?"

"Oh, it's fine doc, go ahead," both men agreed.

"OK, so Old Man, you had a skull fracture and subdural hematoma," she continued. "A neurosurgeon from Bangor had to come up and do brain surgery."

"Oh, so that's what this new zipper is on my scalp then," said the Old Man, smiling and feeling the staples.

"Correct," said Dr. Butler. "Those will come out in the next couple days."

"Oh, I was hoping we could open it up and pour in some new brains," he joked. "Mine are a bit frazzled."

"I'm afraid there's nothing to be done about that," she smiled. "That comes with being a North Woods trapper," she added, patting his hand. "You also lost a lot of blood and were stung by over fifty angry honeybees. It took a lot of Benadryl, prednisone, and IV fluids to get you back on solid ground.

"And... Mr. Baker, you also had a hairline parietal skull fracture but no intracranial bleeding. Your right shoulder kept our general surgeon busy for three hours, sewing up the muscle and skin. And you have a couple broken ribs. But everything should heal fine. Tomorrow you'll both do some physical therapy, and I suspect you'll be headed home in two or three days. Any questions?"

"My wife always says I'm thick skulled, guess it came in handy this time. Has anyone spoken with her? Does she know I'm here?"

"Rae Ann wanted to come immediately, but we told her

you've been comfortably sleeping. She was making arrangements for the kids and plans to come tomorrow. Good night fellas, and try to behave," she said heading out the door.

They finished the vanilla pudding when Ted Thompson came in.

"Hey Sheriff," the two patients said together.

"Wow, good to see you guys awake. I've been coming every couple days to check on you and usually you're both sound asleep."

They all explained their pieces of information to each other regarding the robbery, chase, and fight at the rest stop.

"So, what happened to the One-Eyed Joe gang?" asked Bob.

"Well Mac put two bullet holes in my car door before I killed him. Joe and Slim nearly died from the beating you gave them. Joe is now completely blind, big Joyce had extensive knee surgery, and all three are out of the hospital and in the state prison where they belong. They were wanted for robberies all over California. They'd steal anything they could get their hands on, but mostly beehives, and then drive them far away and sell 'em to people out of town who had no idea they were stolen goods."

"I'm glad those buggers are in jail," sighed the Old Man.

"Me too. Have you talked to Rae Ann?" asked Bob.

"Ayup, I've been giving her updates each day. She's coming tomorrow to pick you up. You know Bob... I have to apologize for misjudging you. I've had this close-minded way of thinking for so many years now. It's hard to break out of it. A stranger with a southern accent and rumor of prison.... I just could not accept that you might be a good guy."

"Thanks," said Bob sincerely. "Apology accepted."

"Old Man, I buried Lou back behind your cabin and arranged for you to stay at the hotel this winter while you recover," said Ted.

"Thanks," said the Old Man. "That's reasonable."

"It's getting late, I'll let you guys get some sleep now," said Ted as he headed for the door.

"Good night," said Bob and the Old Man.

20

BROTHER'S KEEPER

The next morning, they had breakfast followed by two hours of physical therapy, working on balance, grip strength, and range of motion. Dr. Butler stopped in at lunchtime to give them an update.

"Hello gentlemen, the nurses and physical therapy team have given me reports on you two. Progressing nicely. Bob, your wife called to confirm she's on her way and should be here this evening, so you will be free to go," she said looking at Bob. "And you Mr. Old Man," she smiled, "need two more days of R&R, rest and recuperation, along with PT, before Sheriff Ted Thompson will pick you up to go back to Allagash. Sound reasonable?"

Both men nodded. "Thanks for all the help, Doc," said the Old Man.

"Not a problem," she said. "It is enjoyable taking care of nice patients. Good luck and stay out of trouble now, you hear?" She hit the Purell and headed out the door.

The two friends sat quietly for a few minutes after the doctor left. Bob Baker finally broke the silence. "I know I was standoffish about my backstory," he started. "But I was

afraid you may not keep me around if you knew about my past issues."

The Old Man nodded.

"But now we've really been over the trail together," continued Bob, "and I feel comfortable sharing. You've told us your story as well. I realize I have nothing to be ashamed of, it's just tough times and everyone, every family, has 'em eventually... So, it all happened about three years ago. My younger brother Tommy was always a wild one, a non-conformist, fun-loving guy that always seemed to find trouble. Booze and a temper got him into plenty of it. He wouldn't look for fights, but sure wouldn't turn one down either."

The Old Man listened intently from his hospital bed.

"Now if this was fifty years ago, Tommy would have worked in the coal mines like all the other roughnecks in Muhlenberg County, made a living and been fine. But times have changed, those hard workin,' hard livin' coal jobs are long gone. It's like a dark cloud has settled on Appalachia. Folks either go to college and get the heck out, or often fall into pills and crime. Sure there's a few good jobs, but not enough to go around. Tommy spit in the face of authority, just didn't give a darn. The local cops and judges had it in for him because he'd done his dance just outside the law. He'd shown them up in court a time or two as well. They were pretty raw about that. Tommy's no angel like I said, but they were itching to throw the book at him. The judge said next time Tommy stepped outta line, he was going away for a long while. So that got Tommy's attention and he was trying to keep his nose clean for real.

"The feud Tommy has with the law is almost as long as

the feud we Bakers have with the Lewises. A bunch of no-count dirtbags that lived across the holler from us. Four boys and two girls, their own mama couldn't even stand 'em. She split after the last one was born. Lewis Sr. didn't raise 'em, he let 'em run wild and mean as the hogs, curdogs, and fighting cocks on their place. Even when there were good jobs them Lewis boys didn't work. They'd rather steal, cheat, and lazy themselves silly. Bunch of racist jerks too. Anyways, Tommy busted Ron Lewis's nose a month before in a pool hall fight. Thought that was the end of it because everything had been quiet, and Tommy was on best behavior.

"I was supposed to meet Tommy outside of town one Friday evening to fish in Cripple Creek. I figured it was a great way to keep him out of the bars and catch up with him. Well Tommy lost his license years before so was walking out to the creek where we were meeting. Apparently, the Lewis boys saw him walking. Ron Lewis wanted revenge. They saw Tommy had a fishing pole so knew exactly where he was going. They couldn't jump him right along the road where people would see, so they dropped Ron off at the fishing hole with a baseball bat to sit in ambush.

"Tommy had just cast out into the creek and was watching his line. It was nine o'clock at night, middle of the summer, still light out but getting shadowy. Ron Lewis came up behind him and swung the aluminum bat into Tommy's right knee, dropped him to the ground. Ron swung the bat down to crush his skull, but Tommy rolled out of the way and the bat left a huge dent in the ground. Tommy scrambled to his feet and Ron swung the bat at his body. Tommy reflexively deflected it with his left hand and it broke a couple fingers.

He was hurt with basically only one good hand and one good leg left. Ron was going to kill him for the broken nose and embarrassment he'd suffered in the pool hall. The Lewises were always paying off the local judges with drug money, so they knew he'd walk.

"Tommy crowded into the bigger man so he couldn't get a full swing of the bat. Tommy grabbed onto one of the overall straps on Ron's chest with his crippled left hand. The bulky Lewis couldn't shake Tommy free and couldn't smash him with the ball bat. Tommy was struggling to stay on his feet with the injured knee. He knew if he went down the bigger man would stomp on him with boots and bat. It was brutal and Tommy was getting weak. He pulled in close and drew his filet knife, jamming it through the overalls up into Ron's mid-section. He stabbed a few times in desperation and Lewis finally started wilting and shrunk back. That's when I drove up, my truck's headlights lit the scene...

"You stabbed me, you freakin' stabbed me! I heard Ron yell in shock as he stepped back and dropped the bat.

"Jeez, what the heck is going on? I shouted.

"He jumped me! yelled Tommy. *He came out of nowhere,* Tommy wheezed, and looked scared and panicked.

"There was blood all over Tommy's right hand, he stared in horror at what was happening. It was like a disaster unraveling in slow motion before our eyes. Ron Lewis was going quiet and the front of his greasy overalls were turning crimson. In the headlights I could see him going pale. My mind was racing. I heard Tommy yelling, *No! No! No!*

"Ron fell forward gasping, bloody froth at his mouth wetting the summer grass. There were fireflies blinking along the creek. Our frozen shock was interrupted by the sound of a car coming at us from town. The headlights flashed across the road. I grabbed the knife out of Tommy's hand and told him to run.

"*Go through the creek culvert so they don't see you, get over to the rail depot tonight while it's dark, you hear me? Get on a freighter going west and get out of here. Get out west and don't come back for at least a year!* I was practically yelling at him, but it was all so rushed because someone was coming.

"*All right all right*, Tommy gasped. He hobbled down into the creek, headed for the culvert. He looked back at me once and said, *Thanks Bob*, and then he was gone. Just in time too because a truck pulled up into the gravel turnoff. The headlights were on me and it was the rest of the Lewis boys. The first words I heard were, *Did ya git 'em Ronnie?* Then, *What the? Ronnie? What the heck?*

"The rest is all kind of a blur to me. One of the Lewis boys ran down and rolled Ron onto his back.

"*You killed 'em, dang you Baker, you killed Ronnie*! Then he yelled at his brothers to call the cops.

"Time seemed to be rushing in and out. I felt pressure in my head. I was thinking of running. I was thinking of Rae Ann and the kids. I was thinking of Tommy and really felt paralyzed in time and space. Before I knew it, sirens were louder than the chorus frogs and then the flashing red and blue lights of two cop cars and an ambulance washed out the fireflies. The town sheriff told me to freeze – but I had already been that way for what felt like hours. He ran at me and another cop had his pistol drawn. They were yelling at me to drop the knife, but my ears were pulsing and distant. I looked back at the culvert where Tommy last stood, and the lights were reflecting red and blue on the water. They tased me then and it was over.

"I woke up in the Muhlenberg County jail. The case was all pretty clear to the cops and lawyers. The Lewises couldn't act surprised that it was me at the river instead of Tommy because that would have shown that they were involved. I claimed self-defense and with no witnesses or honest judges, I could have gotten off with fines and public service. The Lewises and their cronies claimed that we Bakers had been threatening them with knives before. Our feud is well known to everyone in the area, so this seemed reasonable. They said if someone comes at you with a bat you should run, not stab them to death. It was a mess. A whole lot of legal mumbo jumbo, I didn't understand half of it at the time. We didn't have money for a fancy attorney. The public defender seemed like he was a teenager and got Ds in law school. So...

"I was guilty of involuntary manslaughter and got sentenced to four years in Green River Correctional. Not a pleasant place, I'll tell you that. Lot of bad dudes in there. Some decent guys too. Lot of people with rough upbringings. You hear their stories and it's not surprising that they ended up there. You'd be surprised if they didn't end up there. How can a baby or a little kid turn out to be a "normal" upstanding citizen with some of the things they're exposed to? A lot of the guys in there just had untreated mental illness, a lot of drug issues, and then there were a very few just plain evil characters. Those were the ones to avoid. I read a lot, ran, lifted weights, wrote letters. Minded my own business.

"Rae Ann and the kids came to visit some, but it actually made things worse for me because I always knew they'd have to leave. I hated for them to see me in there like a caged animal. I've told Rae Ann the entire story of what happened at Cripple Creek, but not the kids. We didn't want to put that pressure on them to keep it a secret. If all of this came out, things could blow up again. So, they just know I was protecting myself and things got bad.

"The judge said I could serve half of the sentence for good behavior and get out after two years on parole. While I was locked up the remaining Lewis brothers made it clear that two years in prison was not enough punishment for me. They were also very confused at how they dropped off Ron at the river to club Tommy, and when they came to pick him up Tommy was gone, Ron was dead, and I was there with the murder weapon. Them Lewis boys ain't known for their brains, but they don't believe in magic either."

"Ha," the Old Man chuckled for the first time during this entire intense description. "Well you sure went to bat for your brother, no pun intended."

Bob smiled. "Yeah, I'd do it again too," he said quickly.

"Why don't you just leave Kentucky for good? Get Rae Ann and the kids and move up here?" asked the Old Man excitedly. "Or move anywhere else, just anywhere, get out of Muhlenberg County for good?"

Bob looked thoughtfully at his hospital gown and the picked over lunch tray from the afternoon meal. He wasn't thinking about his response because that was clear to him. It was the reasons for the response that he pondered.

"It's my home, that's where I grew up. Rae Ann's folks are

there and gettin' up in age. The kids' friends are all there. The place has fallen on hard times, that's for sure, I just… I can't leave it to the Lewises to overrun the place. You get rotten apples, or rotten leaders in a place, and they'll mess it up for everyone. I can't just run away from that. Shoot… I feel bad I got out of prison and came up here. It felt good to clear my head though."

"Ayup," exclaimed the Old Man with a smile. "Came up here to clear your head and end up fishing me out of a frozen lake and fighting rogue beekeepers!"

"No kidding," laughed Bob with a shake of his head. "But that's it exactly! Every place has got their problems: Maine, Los Angeles, Louisville, Russia, Benin. You name the place, there's a majority of folks tryin' to hold down the fort and treat others decent, and a few all-out arrogant whack-jobs making things difficult."

The two friends sat quietly for several minutes. The Old Man gazed out of the fifth story window at the parking lot as evening fell. Bob looked out the half-open door to the hospital hall.

"Have you heard from Tommy since then?" asked the Old Man.

"Not directly. We've had to be careful because we know the Lewises are watching everything trying to find him. But Tommy sent a letter to a PO box my cousin has in Atlanta. Tommy is working on a ranch in New Mexico, married a girl from Taos, and they have a one-year-old boy named Bob and another baby on the way."

"Wow, all that in just a few years?" exclaimed the Old Man.

Bob chuckled and shook his head, "Who would have thought... Wild Tommy out of Kentucky, settled down with a family, not touching a drop of liquor."

"Does it make you angry?" asked the Old Man.

"What do you mean?" asked Bob.

"That you had to spend two years behind bars..." the Old Man paused. "Tommy got off easy, fresh start, clean and clear. You got the felony on your record and have to watch your back."

"No," Bob said slowly. "This is truly the best-case scenario. Tommy was headed down a dangerous path. Muhlenberg County is overrun with opioids and other drugs, or maybe the Lewises would have got him? Or some other thing? He had to get out. That night on Cripple Creek was just the perfect scenario to force it into happening. I'd gladly do a couple years in the pen for him to get the rest of his life clean and happy. Well worth it. And I'll be darned if I'm gonna keep runnin' and let the county go down any further. Me and Rae Ann are staying put. We'll do our best to clean the place up, try to get some new jobs in there. How about recreation jobs? No more coal, that's the past, despite what any out-of-touch orange-faced baboon from Washington says. Eastern Kentucky's got hills and rivers and beautiful woods. Solar, wind, reclamation projects, kayaking, camping, miles of hiking. Heck we could even start a camp like Mitch does at Okimachobee!" Bob was really getting fired up now, talking excitedly.

"Ayup, I'm not worried about you Bob. And to tell you the truth, I'm not too worried about Muhlenberg County either," the Old Man said with a big sincere smile on his creased face.

"Thanks," said Bob with moist eyes. "That means a lot to me."

Just then the door opened, and Rae Ann Baker came in, wearing a Cleveland Indians ballcap, wind breaker, and scarf.

"Oh honey!" she said. Seeing her husband in a hospital gown made her cringe. "Hey Old Man."

"I'm fine dear," said Bob, jumping out of bed to give her a big hug and kiss. "See?" as he hid a mild wince.

"Is it really that cold out?" asked the Old Man, looking at her jacket and scarf.

"It is for a southern lady like myself," she said smiling.

"It's so sunny out, I thought it was 70 degrees," questioned the Old Man.

"You've been in here over a week guys, and it's sunny but can't be more than 50. Really feelin' like fall."

While Bob changed into his jeans and t-shirt, Rae Ann walked over to the Old Man and gave him a hug. She looked at the staples on his scalp and just shook her head. "I sent him up here for safety," she said sternly, "and look at what you boys got in to."

"Sorry," said the Old Man with a sheepish smile.

"Now Bob Baker, I'm taking you back to Kentucky and you're not leaving my sight! You hear?" Rae Ann said in a stern southern twang.

"Yes ma'am," said Bob obediently, with the same sheepish smile the Old Man had plastered on his face.

They said their goodbyes and the two men shook hands. Bob was happy to feel the familiar strong grip returning to the old trapper. Bob and Rae Ann gathered his few things in a plastic hospital bag, signed the discharge paperwork, and headed out into the hall.

The Old Man laid back in his quiet hospital bed, pondering all the twists and turns of fate and life seasons in one man's journey. The infinite ways those circumstances intermingle with other people's spheres of existence. He looked out the window to the parking lot below. Red, yellow, and brown leaves blew along the pavement and clumped along the curbs. He saw the couple walking. Bob looked chilled in a t-shirt and held his arms across his chest. Rae Ann had her right arm locked in his left, pulling him close. They got into a green pickup truck with Kentucky plates. If his eyesight was better, he could have seen that they were laughing.

The Old Man got out of bed gingerly and grabbed his jeans from the hospital chair in the corner. He fished out the old leather wallet and flipped past the driver's license and other cards. His leathery fingers trembled and finally got out a small worn piece of paper with a scribbled phone number and the name Ken.

The End

ACKNOWLEDGEMENTS

Thanks to Trisha for being my editor in chief and putting up with my projects. Thanks to our four amazing, fun, nice, talented children who are constantly inspiring me. This project has given me immense respect and admiration for true authors, and especially the "greats", who are able to capture human events, emotions, and meaning into literary form. Like elite athletes, they are able to do what few others can.

If you would like another copy of this book or know someone that may be interested, please email BobBaker.NorthwoodsPublishing@gmail.com for more details.

CPSIA information can be obtained
at www.ICGtesting.com
Printed in the USA
JSHW051120080522
25591JS00003B/6